Instant Heiress

DEEP DARK SECRETS

BOOK TWO

J.J. LOVE

SIMONE FOX

CRAVE PUBLISHING

Instant Heiress

First Print Edition: May 2023

Crave Publishing

Kailua, HI 96734

www.cravepublishing.net

Formatting: Crave Publishing

ISBN-13: 978-1-64034-664-2

CHAPTER 1

Jax

"What can I get ya?" the bartender asks, setting down a napkin in front of me.

"A Jameson on the rocks when you have the chance."

He nods and walks away, tending to a couple on the end in the same manner. Seeing the two make me think of my sister Kylie and Johnathan, and I can't help but feel a pit of jealousy in my gut. It's only been a year since Kylie came to live in Manhattan, and she has already managed to surpass me in every way.

She's moved into Johnathan's huge penthouse, and her career seems to be going well, even after the investigation. Johnathan put her in charge of some departments, and of course she's still his assistant. She even managed to have a kid before me. Mom gave me an earful when she heard the news, and I've been getting interrogated about my own love life ever since. I slump a little in my seat, feeling a bit sorry for myself, and I can't help but wonder… *Is this really how my life is supposed to go?*

A subtle essence alerts my senses, bringing me back to the present as the most incredible woman walks past me and takes a seat a few stools down. The bartender returns with my drink, but I'm too enamored to notice.

Her presence is a little unnerving. She's clearly unlike any of the women I'm used to seeing around here. It's almost like her being in the room makes this a better place. And from the looks she's getting from the other patrons, they seem to agree.

I tear my gaze away before she notices. That's all I need. To be known as the creepy guy at the martini bar. Staring at the iced liquid, I take a sip of my drink and let the alcohol soothe me, eyeing her from my peripherals.

She seems to ignore the attention she draws in effortlessly for the most part, scrolling through her phone. Texts? Social media? Or work? Her green, form-fitting dress and stiletto heels would have me assuming she's here to meet someone. But after working on Johnathan's investigation for so long, I don't take anything at face value anymore.

I watch her the best I can without drawing attention to myself, but she doesn't notice me at all. She begins rubbing her temple with one hand as she continues to scroll through her phone with the other one. I do recognize that look; it's definitely work related.

She adjusts herself slightly as the bartender approaches her. "A glass of red. Samantha, if you have it, please."

My ears perk up at the name. This must be a sign from the universe. I chuckle to myself at the thought while swirling my ice cubes around my glass.

"Something amusing?" I look up from staring at my glass. Is she talking to me? I look around, but we seem to be the only two people at the bar, and the bartender seems to have disappeared for the moment.

"Yes…I was talking to you." She smiles in a way that almost makes me forget my name.

"Uh, yes, I mean no." She laughs a little clearly amused by this dumb idiot who can't put two words together. "Just thinking about something." I try quickly to recover from the horrible first impression I'm clearly giving off.

"Well?" The bartender returns just in time, setting a glass of the house red wine in front of her. It gives me a minute to gather my thoughts.

"Oh, it was nothing. Nothing important, anyway." I clear my throat so I don't sound like a sixteen-year-old boy. Catching me off guard seems to have caused my voice to go up a few octaves. Which I didn't know was actually possible.

"I see." She turns back to her phone.

"Actually, I couldn't help but overhear your wine choice." I turn to face her.

"What about it?" she says, her voice short as she turns her attention back to me. Her thick lips grip the edge of her glass as she takes another drink, and I clear my throat again before continuing.

"Samantha is the name of my niece. I thought a wine named after her would be a nice present for my sister."

"Oh." Her eyes are so piercing I can almost feel her trying to touch my soul. I can tell she's trying to get a read on me. Not that it would matter anyway; she's definitely way out of my league. "Well, this isn't it. But there's a red wine from Samantha's Winery. Probably the best wine I've ever had."

"Really?" I can't believe she's actually talking to me. "Where's it from? Jersey? Philly?"

"Ireland, actually." The faintest smirk appears on her face.

Every word she speaks puts me farther under her spell. Only then do I notice her subtle accent, as if she's trying to hide it from the rest of the world. I can't help but want to know more.

As I become brave enough to search her eyes, I can clearly see there are secrets behind them. I mean we all have our secrets. But something about the look behind her eyes makes her secrets seem endless.

"I could tell you weren't from around here."

"Oh really?" She continues to stare. "And what gave you that impression?"

"There's just something about you that doesn't fit this place. New York, I mean."

"Well, that's a relief. And here I was thinking I blended in so well."

I try to keep my eyes from trailing down her body. "I don't think that's possible."

The bartender returns with another drink for me. She's either sneaky or the bartender is way ahead of me because I don't remember ordering another drink.

"Let me guess. As a native New Yorker, what would you offer me? A tour of the city?"

She's baiting me. I can see it in her eyes that she's waiting for me to slip up so she can destroy me with her rejection. But I'm not one to give up so easily. Especially against a woman like her. I've got nothing to lose here.

"Well, sorry to disappoint you. But I'm not from New York. I'm a foreigner. Just like you."

"Just like me, huh?" There's that smirk again. God, she's sexy. The way her legs are crossed hikes her dress up in ways that make me want to explore more.

She averts her eyes as she takes another sip, clearly done with her examination of me. My fingers wrap around my drink, and I let the cold feeling of the whiskey cool my throat.

This seems to be going well. Maybe I'll even get

her name and number by the end of the night. I turn to restart the conversation and do my best not to choke as I see my beautiful temptress turn to stand.

My heart hammers as she glides toward me and leans in to whisper in my ear. “It’s too crowded in here. I have a hotel room nearby if you’re interested in getting more acquainted.”

Wait, she’s not a hooker, is she? God, I can’t ask her that; in the remote chance she’s not, I’d ruin everything. That’s not a question a woman takes lightly.

I will take the chance either way. Observing this woman has me the most intrigued I’ve been in a very long time. And I miss it. I miss this feeling of excitement in my life.

Since Johnathan’s case, I’ve had so much work dumped on me that’s been my entire existence. I’ve clearly forgotten there’s a whole different fascinating world out there, if you just take a chance to find it.

The universe sent me this chance, and I’m gonna take it. “I’ll handle the check and meet you outside.”

CHAPTER 2

Amelia

We meet right outside of the bar, which is across the street from my hotel. I hadn't planned on taking a stranger back to my room tonight, but hey, I've had a lot on my plate and could use the break. Plus, he's hot, so it could be a good time.

When he finally comes out, he's pushing his hair back away from his face, and I see his eyes searching for me on the side of the sidewalk. When he finally spots me, his face lights up, and it makes me laugh to myself. He's like a puppy—innocent and naive to the dangerous waters he's currently treading in.

I'm never one to show off my true self—the person that I really am under my sheep's clothing. But sometimes it's tempting to see how people would react to knowing how much of a devil I can be. But that's all wishful thinking and something alcohol likes to tempt me with. In the grand scheme of things, telling anyone anything, especially a man like him who had no business in my world, would only end in disaster.

"Ready to go?" he asks me as soon as he reaches me, offering his arm before we cross the street.

I let him lead me, knowing that if I allow him to take the reins a little bit before we get upstairs, giving him a false sense of security that he's in charge, it will make dominating him that much sweeter.

I wave to the doorman as we pass by, giving him a subtle nod when he shifts his hand down to his waistband where I know a Glock is hiding underneath his suit jacket. It's kind of cute how protective they are sometimes.

He relaxes when I flash him a wink, folding his arms back in front of his waist before turning away from me to face the door again.

"So how long are you staying here?" the man asks me. I still haven't gotten his name yet, but I don't really care to, either. He's just an anonymous hookup, after all.

I doubt I'll ever see him again after this.

"Not long." I tap the button on the elevator when we step inside of it. "Yourself?"

He rubs the back of his neck with his hand, watching the doors close and seal us inside. "I'm not sure yet."

"Hm." I hum. I can't tell if he's fishing for me to

ask him for more details or if he's not interested in talking about it anymore.

I'll admit, I'm not in the mood to play therapist for a hookup. Some girls may find that sexy, but I don't. I only want my men whimpering when they're underneath me and too over-stimulated to form coherent sentences other than begging my name.

It's not my job to make sure that every man I come into contact with feels safe and heard. If they wanted that, they could go to a strip club and pay a stripper to listen to them bitch and moan about their lives for a while.

The door pings open when we reach my floor, and I quickly tug him out of the elevator before he can actually start whining. I'm so pent up that I need to expel some kind of energy, and he just so happens to be exactly my type.

Actually, now that I think about it, his tie could make for a great gag.

Smirking to myself, I let go of his arm to dig through my purse to find my keycard. He waits patiently next to me while I fish it out and swipe it on the pad next to the door. I shoulder it open, flicking on the lights and stepping inside.

It's a nice hotel room and gives me a great view of the street down below of the outside of the building. I haven't had much time to canvas while I'm up here, spending way too much time tracking down shipments while jumping from phone call to phone call in between deals.

It's a fucking hassle, but it's part of the job. And no one but myself is going to get this shit moving if I'm not the one pulling the strings behind the scenes.

I let him into my apartment, throwing the lock back into place the second he steps in. Right as he's about to open his mouth to talk again, I grab him by the front of his shirt and pin him against the door.

His eyes widen at me. "Uh—"

I cut him off by sealing my lips against his.

His hands find my hips, squeezing them while he pulls me in closer so that our bodies are pressed flushed together. I can already feel how hard he is underneath those tailored slacks of his, the head of his cock practically poking me right in the stomach.

I grab onto the front of his suit jacket and strip it off of him, leaving it a crumbled mess on the floor. Next comes his shirt, where I tug it roughly out from his pants before quickly moving up to unbutton the first few sets and run my hands over the hard lines of his toned stomach. He groans against my lips, his own hands roaming over my body while he explores it.

Not wanting him to get too far into this just yet, I pull away from him and wrap my hand around his tie. I tug on it and start walking backward, using it as a leash to lead him further into my hotel room and over to where the bed is.

His eyes track me as we move, his Adam's apple bobbing underneath the taut hold I have around his neck. Maybe if he's good, I'll actually let him get off instead of using him for my own self pleasure and kicking him out once I'm satisfied.

It wouldn't be the first time I used a man until I was good and done and not caring one bit if he got off or not too. They had hands for a reason, and if they didn't impress me, they'd be taking care of themselves on the cab ride home back to their own place.

Once we are close enough to the bed, I let go of his tie and grab at the front of his shirt again, using it to turn us around and shove him down onto the bed. His eyes widen slightly when his back hits the mattress, his muscular body bouncing on it slightly.

"Damn, you like it rough or something?" He sits up onto his elbows.

I smirk and push him all the way back down before crawling on top of him to straddle him. "Or something."

I'm in a good mood tonight, not to mention horny as hell. I haven't had a man under me in months; with trying to coordinate this fucking deal, it's getting in the way of my personal life.

My hips grind down onto his, pulling a moan from his lips. "Damn…"

He grabs at me again, finding my waist and holding me while he moves under me. I watch as his eyes slide closed, already getting lost in the pleasure of having me on top of him.

No, this won't do. This is my bedroom to control.

I untangle myself from him and push off of his chest to slide off the bed. His eyes snap open the second I start moving, his hands trying to futilely hold onto me before I can get very far. I turn my back to him and wander over to one of my bags I have yet to unpack still and bend to pick it up.

"Uh," he says, the bed behind me shifting. "You okay?"

"Mmm," is all I respond with.

I toss the bag onto the bench next to the closet and rip it open. There are plenty of miscellaneous items in here that I have yet to use but I figured I'd take around with me anyways, such as an extra tablet, holsters for my Glock, and whatever else random I could think to bring with me overseas.

I dig through the contents and pull out a pair of handcuffs, police-grade, with the keys stuck in the keyhole.

I unlock them and pull the keys out, grinning to myself.

Perfect.

Coming back over to the bed, his eyes immediately zero in on the cuffs, only darting away for a second when I toss the keys onto the nightstand next to him before coming back to focus on them.

"You...want me to handcuff you?"

I laugh before crawling back on top of him, pushing him back down again. "No."

He blinks at me when I grab one of his wrists and trap it inside of a cuff. He doesn't fight me at all when I bring it up and loop the loose side through one of the bars on the frame of the bed and then grab his other wrist and trap it with the other cuff.

He looks up at the cuffs curiously, tugging at them a few times to test their hold.

"You like this kind of thing?" His eyes finally find mine again.

I smirk. "Yeah, you got a problem with that?"

"No, just never done this before." I can tell by the look on his face he's not sure if he should be enjoying this or terrified at being handcuffed by a stranger in a place where nobody knows he went.

Oh, I love to hear that. It's not often that I find a newbie, especially one who seems so willing to entertain my sexual appetite like he does.

I unbutton the rest of his shirt and pull it apart to expose his torso. He's quite ripped for someone who looks like they sit behind a desk all day—which I guess adds to the appeal. It's kind of like me, where my appearance doesn't exactly match who I really am.

"You want to see something?" I ask him, leaning back so I can tug the edge of my dress up my thigh slowly.

He watches me, nodding without saying another word, seemingly paralyzed with either fear or anticipation.

Lifting my hips, I slide it up slowly over my thighs, exposing my skin inch by inch at an agonizingly slow pace. He shifts his hips under me, rubbing the line of that hard cock against my inner thigh as he does so.

When I finally pop the dress over my hips, he groans.

"Fuck…"

"You like? I ask, running my hands over my bare pussy. I didn't bother wearing underwear tonight, knowing that this dress would make it ride up my ass anyway.

He nods quickly, licking his lips. Without thinking, he tugs at the handcuffs, stilling for a moment when he remembers he can't reach out and touch me. It makes me giddy, knowing that he wants to so badly but can't.

I love being a tease.

His cock twitches against my thigh, begging to be let out from the confines of his pants. I sink back down onto him and roll my hips against his, giving him a little bit of a reward for being so obedient.

He groans again. "Shit…"

"You going to cum already?" I let the sarcasm drip from my tone, testing him.

He shakes his head quickly. "No, just…I've never met anyone like you… You're so sexy."

That has me laughing. Oh, I know I am. That's never been a question or an issue for me. In fact, I use it to my advantage quite often to get what I want. Why shouldn't I use the assets I was born and blessed with?

Taking my dress off completely, I toss it onto the floor and let him take me in. This is the only time he'll be able to have a girl like me get in bed with him, so I might as well let him savor every moment of it.

I know for a fact he'll be thinking about me for the next few years, because I know it will be the best sex he's ever had. I will make sure of it.

I take mercy on him finally and unbuckle his belt, freeing him from his pants. His cock springs out, rock hard and already leaking precum at the tip.

"Aw." I tap it with my finger.

"What can I say?" His voice is strained. "You're hot…"

"I know."

He chuckles. "I like the confidence."

Wrapping a hand around his cock, I stroke it a few times, seeing more precum leak out. "You want me that bad, huh?"

"Yes," comes his immediate answer.

I smile a little. I can appreciate the honesty. He tugs at his cuffs again, squirming under me when I keep stroking him. I guess I should stop torturing him and get on with it—I'm horny too.

Not bothering to pull his pants down any further, I lift myself up and line myself over the tip of his cock. I don't want to waste any more time on prep, even if it might hurt a little. I don't mind a little pain with my pleasure, anyway.

I slide down onto him, earning a strangled gasp as my walls hug his cock tight.

"Ohhhh fuck…"

It's a tight squeeze, but it feels sooo fucking good. As soon as I have him all the way in, I sit there for a moment to adjust to his size. He's not small by any means and fits perfectly inside, like he was somehow made for me.

The cuffs clink against the frame of the bed as he fights their hold. I love that he's so desperate to touch me and can't. I'm completely in control of this situation, and there's nothing he can do about it.

Finally I start moving, and I roll my hips a few times, testing how deep he is inside of me before lifting my hips up and slamming down on top of him.

"Shit!" he barks out, his head falling back onto the pillow under him. "Ohhh fuck."

I ride him, my hips slamming down onto his cock over and over again until we're both panting heavily. I missed this—having a man completely prone under me. It's so fucking hot when they're begging and squirming, trying to hold on while I use them like my own personal sex doll.

He seems to enjoy it though, given the way his hips are trying to buck up into mine to get as deep as he can inside of my pussy. His cock is already pulsating inside of me, ready to explode.

"You want to cum?" I ask him, resting my hands on his chest.

"Fuck—" His eyes squeeze shut.

"Tell me." I throw my head back, letting my hair tickle the curve of my ass. "Tell me how much you want it."

"I want it so bad," he groans.

If it were any other day, I'd deny him and tell him no. Torture him a little bit before I am finally done with him. But tonight, I'm in a good mood. Plus, he hasn't fought me on any of this or giving me back talk about getting handcuffed, so I suppose I can let him get off with me.

I let my body do all the work, giving in to my instincts as I ride him, my walls tingling as they clamp around him. I'm so wet I can feel the juices flowing down around his balls. When I cum, my nails dig into his pecs, a moan leaving my lips as I ride through my orgasm.

Warmth spills into me, his cum dripping out of me and smearing over his abs while I continue to move my hips against his. I want to ride out my orgasm for as long as possible, his dick hitting me in all the right spots that I cum again right before I finally collapse onto his chest.

He's panting hard under me, his heart pounding in my ear.

"Wow," is all he says when he finally catches his breath.

I smirk to myself.

What can I say, I'm great in bed.

I ROLL over the next morning, wincing when the sunlight hits my face and blinds me. A groan escapes my lips, quickly cut off by the pillow I take from under my head and place over my face to block out the assault on my eyes.

How did I forget to draw the curtains back before I went to bed? My routine was always so precise, I never tended to miss a step—

Next to me, the bed shifts.

Oh, that's right.

Pushing the pillow off of my face, I turn my head to look at the man sleeping under my sheets. His muscular back faces me, bare of any markings from my nails—which I know can't be said for the state of his chest.

The memory makes me smirk to myself. I had to admit, he'd been a good lay. Surprising me with how down he was about everything I'd thrown at him. Who knew some random guy at the bar could be kinky just like me?

But him staying overnight was...unexpected. I had two giant meetings to get to this morning, and staying in bed to wait for him to wake up so we could do something domestic like have breakfast together made me cringe internally.

It was safe to say I never had the mindset to

become a housewife or some girl at the bar who brought a guy home and slowly fell in love with him. That wasn't my style. I much preferred feeling the weight of a gun in my hand and aiming it at a sweaty forehead of a man who begs for his life before I pull the trigger.

Am I a little sadistic? Sure, but who isn't in this business?

Sliding out of bed as carefully as I can, I make my way over to my bathroom to take a quick shower. Hopefully by the time I'm out, he'll get the hint and leave. Or…better yet, maybe come join me for a nice little shower fuck before I actually kick him out.

Unfortunately, I'm a little disappointed when he doesn't show and even more so when I finally get out and see him still sleeping. Maybe I wore him out a little more than I thought I did last night. We did get pretty rough, but again, he seemed to be really into it.

Who knows? There was the possibility of last night being his first time in a while. Maybe he needed to build up his stamina again.

Which isn't my problem.

Getting dressed quietly, I fix myself in the mirror and make sure I look exactly like the vixen I am before heading back over to the bed. I fish out a few bills and set them down onto the side table next to his side with a full glass of water from the tap. I doubted he needed money for a cab, but this is my little way of saying, "Thanks for the great night," because it really was.

It isn't every day a man lets you completely destroy him and then ask for more. Especially without all of the questions and when can we see each other again type of nonsense. That's a different kind of special.

I take one last look in the mirror before heading out, letting the door shut soundly behind me.

CHAPTER 3

Jax

WHEN I TURN my head and notice that the bed next to me is empty, I frown.

I roll onto my back slowly, wincing at how sore my body is. It feels good though—the same kind of sore you get after a really intense workout. It's satisfying and makes me sigh softly to myself while I let my mind roll through the memories of my mystery woman and how hard we both got off.

Who knew I'd picked up a kinky one, not to mention one who clearly seemed way out of my league? Not that I'm complaining because that was the hottest sex I'd ever had in my entire life.

Opening my eyes, I look up and catch sight of the handcuffs still wrapped around the bed posts above me and smile to myself. I never knew I was into the "no touching/touch me and get punished" kind of sex, but it had been hot to see her take control like that.

She'd practically used me as a sex toy, and for some reason that turned me on even more. She's taken exactly what she wanted from me and had been proud to do it.

I groan softly to myself, feeling my cock harden at the memories of her staring down at me, demanding that I cum. My hand travels down my belly to where my cock lays half hard, and I take it between my fingers and squeeze.

It's been a while since I had sex with someone, and no one's ever come close to how much last night turned me on.

Letting go of my hard cock, I sit up slowly to look around the room, seeing no trace of my mystery woman.

She must've left then.

I try not to let the thought deflate me. I know it's the hopeless romantic in me hoping that a one-night stand would stick around and have breakfast with me or go and grab a cup of coffee before we parted ways. I wish we could've exchanged numbers before she left though, even if it was just for a repeat of last night.

Sighing, I slide the covers off myself and head to the shower to wash the night off of my skin. Honestly, it might have been a good thing for her to just leave. No sense in getting attached to a stranger, let alone when I'm already so buried in my work that I can barely breathe most days.

I don't have time for any kind of relationship, even if it's a friends-with-benefits type deal.

Once I'm finally clean and dried off, I collect my clothes from the night before. Weirdly enough, it feels like I'm doing some kind of walk of shame putting the same clothes on that had been torn off me the night before. Checking my watch, I didn't exactly have any time to spare before I needed to head back to the office, so hopefully no one was going to call me out on my recurring outfit.

Heading back over to the bed to do one final sweep, I catch sight of a few bills placed under the edge of a glass of water.

Did she...*pay* me for last night?

I try to force back the complete disappointment.

Wow. Now I really feel like a cheap whore.

Shaking my head, I leave the money there and force my feet into my shoes before taking off. Thinking back to my night, I try to run through my memories while I step into the elevator and stab the ground-floor button.

Did she not have a good time? I remember very distinctively her getting off too, so what the fuck was the money about? Did I look poor to her?

All of these thoughts fire me up and frustrate me to no end. If she had that much money to throw around, she should've recognized I'd been dressed expensively. It wasn't like this suit was made of cheap materials and didn't fit properly.

As the elevator slows to a stop and the doors pop

open, I push through the small crowd of people waiting to get inside and head out through the lobby.

Whatever, it's not like I'll ever see her again. So why am I so caught up in what she thought of me?

I need to get laid more often—that's the real issue. Why put all of my energy into a woman that clearly only viewed this as a transactional thing and not a fun experience the both of us shared together?

Getting out onto the street, I locate my car and slide into the front seat after unlocking it. Thankfully, there are no tickets stuck to my front windshield even though the parking sign a few feet from me clearly states I've overstayed my welcome.

Checking my blind spot, I start my car and pull out onto the street. I'm ready to drown myself in work for the next few hours and pretend like last night never happened at all. It's easier to push down my feelings than to keep reminiscing and making myself feel worse about myself.

It's not that I don't have the potential to grab a hot woman and bring her back to my place—I know I'm good looking, and I have plenty of money to spoil whoever I want. I hate that my mind keeps circling back to my mystery woman even though I don't even know her name.

What sense does that make?

I sigh when my speakers chime with an incoming call. Tapping on the screen on the center console, I answer.

“Yeah.”

Over the speakers, my sister snorts. “What? *That’s* how you’re going to greet me?”

Kylie…of course she’d be calling me first thing in the morning.

“Sorry, haven’t had my coffee yet.”

“Clearly…”

I flick my eyes over to my rear facing mirror, checking before I merge into the lane next to me to get into the passing lane. “Did you need something?”

“Well, no. I just wanted to call and check up on you.”

That had me raising my brow. “Why?”

It’s not that I don’t appreciate my sister calling me to do that; it just seems out of the blue. Our lives have been so busy lately, what with me trying to put the pieces back together with the Ronsberry disaster and her figuring out her relationship with Johnathan, that I really didn’t expect her to keep up with me.

There would never be any hard feelings when it came to my sister trying to live her life—I *wanted* her to. She deserves to be happy, no matter who she ends up with. Johnathan is my best friend, so I know he’ll take care of her.

Especially after we went to hell and back for him.

“You seem…off lately.”

“Off? How so?”

I can practically hear her shrugging. “I don’t know. Maybe sad? Lonely?”

I groan. "Please tell me you're not calling to give me love advice."

"What's wrong with that?" she challenges. "Why can't I be concerned with my brother's happiness?"

A laugh escapes me. "I didn't say you couldn't. But I don't need the advice. I'm fine."

Well, I *was* fine until I discovered that stack of cash next to the bed this morning. Remembering it makes my blood boil. Too bad I didn't have my mystery woman's number or else I'd call her and ask her what the fuck.

Kylie groans at me. "Jax, come oooon. Talk to me. I'm your favorite sister. You have an obligation to tell me these things."

I roll my eyes. "First off, you're my *only* sister. Second, I'm fine. I promise."

"You don't seem fine. Like I said, you seem sad."

My foot taps the brake when traffic slows in front of me, the light up ahead changing from yellow to red. My car idles quietly, making me feel the need to tap my fingers along the steering wheel. I've never been good with silence; it's always made me weirdly jittery for some reason.

Whenever I'm in my office going through documents and putting together case files, I always have something going on in the background—whether that be music or the sounds of the city below coming from my open window.

It's an unpopular opinion, but the hustle and bustle of the city has always brought me a strange amount of comfort. Usually, residents take painstaking measures to keep the noise at bay and their living spaces quiet, but for me, I'm the complete opposite.

I roll Kylie's words through my mind, going over them a few times while we both sit in awkward silence. She's not exactly wrong, but not exactly right either.

While I'm not sad or lonely, I do feel rather lost lately. The situation with Ronsberry changed me in some way that I still can't put my finger on.

But whatever it is, it's made me reevaluate a lot of things: namely my career choice.

"I don't know." I sigh. "I'm not sure. I think I'm getting bored."

"Of what?"

"My job, mostly."

She gasps. "Wait what?! Why?"

I flick my turn signal on when the light shifts back to green, moving over to the next lane to get back over to the next block.

"I don't know. Just feeling restless, I guess."

"Anything I can help with?"

"Not really. Just need to figure out what I want to do in life. Can't really make work my hobby when it's already my job."

She giggles. "Wow, who are you and what have you done with my brother? I've never heard you not want to make work your entire life."

Her words have me wincing. Sure, I know she's

joking but there's some definite truth to them. I hate that that's how she perceives me, and she's not wrong either. I *have* made work my life since I had nothing else going on.

My career working for the district attorney isn't one to bat an eye at—in fact, it's a prestigious accomplishment than any one my age would be more than proud to brag about. I thought at the time when I was appointed that my life would finally feel fulfilled. I'd been working tirelessly to move through the ranks, push my way through college and then grad school and then my firm, all the way up until I was in the running to be appointed.

But now that I've been in this role for a little over two years, it's become stagnant. I feel like the entire world is spinning on and moving without me while I'm stuck living behind a desk.

And none of this really hit me until my sister got involved with Johnathan and I got to watch their love blossom.

It's shitty to be jealous of your sister and her happiness, but no one ever claimed for feelings to make sense.

"I know," I finally say. "I need to figure myself out."

"Are you going to quit?"

"No. I don't know. I've only been feeling this way recently."

"I'm sorry, Jax. You know I'm always here for you if you want to talk about it."

I smile. "I know. I appreciate it. Why don't we have dinner together this weekend?"

"I'd love that!"

I chuckle. "Okay, I'll see you then."

"Okay!"

As the call drops, I sag back into my seat and sigh.

Figure myself out…

Yeah, so easy to say and much harder to do.

CHAPTER 4
Amelia

"WHAT DO you *mean* the meeting's canceled?" I growl into my phone.

The man on the other end, some low-level scum that I don't give a damn about talking down to, stutters back at me. "W-well, ma'am, we were just informed today that—"

"Does your boss have any idea what it's cost me just to come over here? You know what, why don't you tell him I'll be taxing that onto his payment?"

"M-ma'am, please—"

I'm gripping the phone so hard in my hand that it hurts. "I'm not in the mood to listen to your excuses. Either he shows his face tomorrow or I'm coming over there and putting a few bullet holes into that chest of his. Think you can pass along that message?"

He chokes out a quick "yes" before the other line goes dead.

I roll my eyes, throwing my phone back into the

passenger seat. Fuck them, honestly. They're all a waste of time dealing with and really just a means to an end. Unfortunately, without this meeting, I won't be guaranteed an audience with my real target.

Honestly, all of this just pisses me off to no end.

It's been a long day. I'm already dealing with enough on my plate; I don't need the added stress of a buyer playing hard to get when I'm not in the mood to be playing any games at all in the first place. See, this is the problem with men who think owning a few racks of guns suddenly gains them authority. It starts going to their head and then all of a sudden they think they're big shots who don't have time for anyone else but with their own self interests.

It pisses me off not only having to deal with those kinds of people but to sell to them too. What I really want is to be able to go back home as soon as possible and get back to my family while I still have time.

The thought suddenly drains me.

Time is such a bastard. It steals so much from you when you least expect it. First my dad, then my brother and now my mother…all of them slipping between my fingers before I ever had the chance to say goodbye.

I hate death.

In this business, it's as common as breathing. But my family's been hit with it particularly hard and in ways we all least expected.

My body feels restless—all of my pent-up anger

from before when I'd gotten the call that my meeting had been canceled is slowly starting to fade to sadness. An emotion I hate. I'd much rather focus on anger instead.

Grabbing onto the rearview mirror, I look over my appearance, adjusting my wig and fixing my eye makeup. I'd spent over an hour crafting up this identity so my buyer wouldn't recognize me and it seems like such a waste to drive back to my hotel room and take it all off.

Glancing out my window again, I watch the front of the bar that I was supposed to be meeting the buyer at. You know what? I might as well blow off some steam. After all, it would be such a waste to let the way this dress looks on me go to waste.

Popping the door to my car open, I grab my purse and hip-check it closed before heading across the street. It's the same bar I was at yesterday, so hopefully there are some good-looking men ready to spend a couple twenties on me to buy me drinks.

After thinking back to last night and how much I miss a man under me, not to mention it's my favorite way to relieve stress, I can't help but have a small hope that maybe my stranger from last night is already inside. I could really go for a round two right about now.

The crowd is a little less lively tonight, and instead of seeing people crowded around the bar waving their credit cards around trying to get the attention of the bartender, all I see are a few guys sitting on stools looking up at the TV overhead playing some basketball game.

I make my way over to it, taking a seat right in the middle so I at least grab the attention of one of them by the time I have my purse resting in my lap. A drink appears in front of me a few moments later, and a man who is relatively handsome is leaning over to make conversation with me.

He's not bad looking by any means, but as soon as he gets close enough, I flinch back from him with how horrible his breath smells.

Good god, I'm not letting that mouth anywhere near my pussy.

I wave him off, quickly thanking him for the drink before sliding off my stool and heading over to the other side of the bar. There is a small group in the back playing pool together and a few stragglers hanging out around them waiting for a turn to crack at a few balls.

On the other side is another small sitting area with another game on the TV, this time some kind of golf tournament, and a few old men crowded around a tall high-top table.

Damn, is tonight going to be a total dud?

That plummets my mood even further. It isn't like I'm not accustomed to taking care of myself every so often, especially when being on the road. But damn, can't a girl get laid?

I slump down into one of the benches on the opposite side of the bar in a dark corner and set my drink down on top of the table. A sigh leaves me, catching the look of a couple next to me who give me a sympathetic look. Great, they probably think I got stood up.

Just as I'm about to get up and call it a night, the front door to the bar opens up and another man walks in—this time one that's very familiar.

The guy from last night.

I grin to myself. Perfect.

He wanders into the bar with a long coat over his suit that practically touches the floor. One hand is stuck in the pocket at his hip while the other is raised to wave to the bartender. He settles down on one of the stools—the same one I was in before, funny enough—and orders himself a drink.

I watch him as he leans on the counter, nursing his drink when it's given to him and striking up a conversation with the man with the bad breath. A smile breaks out over my face when he jumps back suddenly, most likely catching a whiff of the other man's breath.

I chew on my straw, captured by the man who I bedded last night. I'm not going to lie, it was a good lay. A great one, in fact. He'd been so willing to let my take control, only fighting me on it a few times before I got him right where I wanted him.

I love a man who can take orders, especially a man who looks like how my stranger does—hot and put together and with a wild side you wouldn't expect at all just from looking at him.

He finally slides off the stool and wanders away from the bar, spotting me instantly when he scans his eyes around. I pretend not to see him, letting him come to me. I look different today with my makeup and the dark wig I chose to wear for my meeting, so if he recognizes me, I'll be surprised.

I look over when a drink is set down on my table and am pleasantly surprised when my stranger stands in front of me.

"Hey."

I tilt my head at him. Should I play dumb? It would certainly add to the fun of all this. Who knew if we'd see each other again after tonight, so why not spice it up and make it sexy?

"Hello."

He pulls the chair on the opposite side out and takes a seat, running his eyes carefully over me. "I like your hair."

My hand wraps around my glass, lifting it up so I can take a sip from my straw while I think on how to play this. Normally I don't bother with the games or the bullshit and get right to the point of bringing a man back to my room. But after the day I've had, tonight I need to have some fun.

"Thank you. You come here often?"

He lets out a guilty-sounding laugh. "No, not really… I was just over this way again, so I figured why not stop in?"

So he works in the city. Interesting.

Judging by his expensive suit and the way he

carries himself, he makes money and lots of it. Wall Street investor? Stock broker? Something high profile.

"What about you?" he asks. "Do you come here often?"

Instead of answering that, I say, "You know, I never caught your name."

He grins at me. "Jax, and you?"

I narrow my eyes at him, running the edge of the straw around my tongue a few times and capturing his attention while he watches it closely. See, *he* is who I'd let around my pussy. At least I know he has a clean mouth.

"Emma," is the name I finally decide upon.

"Well, Emma." His eyes glancing down at my glass before going right back to my lips. "Why don't I buy you another drink?"

CHAPTER 5

Jax

I HAD A VERY LONG EXHAUSTING day, and I couldn't believe my luck when I saw my mystery woman across the bar. Obviously I was hoping she'd be there which is why I stopped by on my way home, but it was really just a shot in the dark.

And it even got better when she told me her name…Emma. I would have never pegged her for an Emma, but I couldn't care less what her name was; at least this time I had a name. Which made me feel a little bit closer to finding out who she really was.

She had been consuming my thoughts since this morning, and it was actually kind of nice to think about something other than work. So when I saw her, it was almost a relief. An escape from my current reality, a reality that I really didn't want to deal with right now.

Apparently she must be struggling with her own

reality because this time she looked different. A dark wig, different makeup, but one thing she couldn't change was her essence. She could change her looks as much as she wanted but there was no way to change that... Iit was unique. And the energy coming from her was undeniably addicting to me and every other breathing man in the room. There was no hiding it.

After some small talk and witty banter, my mystery woman—Emma—brings me back to her hotel room.

It starts off the same way it did last time, with her trapping me against the door and kissing me. I run my hands all over her body, happy that I finally get to touch her this time around. I had no idea she'd handcuff me to her bed like that, so I didn't get a chance to savor the feel of her under my hands before I lost it.

She lets me hike up her dress and grab her ass, this time wearing a lace pair of underwear that I can't help snapping the band of a few times.

When she pulls away, she grabs my tie again just like last time and leads me to the bed. I'm tossed onto it with little care and have to quickly toe off my shoes and suit jacket before she's already crawling on top of me.

"Eager, aren't we?" she teases.

Whatever this game is, I like it.

She doesn't bother with stripping me any further, strangely enough, and is quick to handcuff me to the frame of the bed again. My wrists are still a little raw from tugging at the metal last night, but not enough for it to hurt too badly.

She sits on my waist, teasing me with a show of pulling her dress down over her chest and showing off her incredible tits. I lick my lips at the sight, wanting so badly to lean forward and wrap my mouth around one of those perky nipples.

Without meaning to, my hips buck under her, my cock hard and strained against the inside of my pants.

She tsks at me and grabs at my tie, tugging at it to use as some sort of leash. I have no idea why but the thought of her trying to choke me to keep me from misbehaving is so hot.

Who am I? Who knew I was into this kind of thing?

Maybe it's always been there, hidden underneath the surface. I'd always been the dominant one in bed for obvious reasons, but with someone like Emma controlling the situation, I could easily see myself falling back and letting her have her way with me.

"Behave," she tells me.

I nod quickly.

She lightens her hold on my tie but still keeps her hand wrapped around it just in case. I watch her play with one of her nipples, squeezing it a few times to tease me again. Fuck, she really knows what she's doing, doesn't she?

How often does she have guys tied up to her bed, at the mercy of her whims?

"You want to be inside me, baby?" she coos.

Oh, fuck…

I nod quickly. I'm so desperate, which I'm sure shows on my face because she laughs. "Aww."

My toes curl while I try to remain still and not accidentally buck up into her again. As much as the idea of being choked turns me on, I want to be inside of her way more.

It's like she senses this because she tugs off her dress and tosses it onto the floor and then leans back to pull my belt apart. I gasp when she finally exposes my cock, her hands working quickly to stroke me and spread the precum already dripping out of my tip.

Fuck, I've never been so turned on in my damn life.

But instead of sliding me inside of her like she did last time, she lets go of my cock so that it falls back onto my belly. Lowering herself down, she rubs her pussy against me, moving her hips in a sensual way while my cock disappears and reappears between her folds.

Shit, that's so hot.

"Mmm, you're so hard for me," she groans, her hand coming up to squeeze one of her tits. "You want me, baby?"

I nod quickly. "So bad."

"You going to be good for me?"

My eyes squeeze shut. Why the fuck am I getting so turned on by this?

A tug around my neck has me opening my eyes again. She pulls at my tie, forcing me to answer her.

"Yes," I finally say.

"Good boy."

A shiver races down my spine at her words.

Without warning, she lifts her hips up and slams down onto me. I choke out a groan, wanting to let myself fall back into the mattress, but the tight hold around my neck keeps me from doing so. She rides me at a punishing pace, using me the way she would a sex toy.

I do everything in my power not to cum, concentrating on pleasing her as much as I can while she uses me. I've never been in this kind of situation before, with someone taking whatever they wanted without apology.

Usually when I'm in bed with a woman, I make sure it's all mutual. I take care of her and make her feel wanted. I go through painstaking lengths to make sure that the sex is good for both of us.

But this, it's anything but.

She's taking exactly what she wants, using me as a vessel for her pleasure. She keeps the tie tight in her hand as she rides me, watching me with a lustful expression.

"Don't cum," she tells me, her walls already tightening around me.

Oh fuck, is she serious?

"Did you hear me?"

I nod quickly. "I won't."

I've never been into delayed orgasm, finding the process much too tedious. But when her pussy clamps down around mine and I feel her walls fluttering around me, trying to milk my cock, I suddenly get it.

It feels incredible, even though my balls are going to absolutely burst.

A groan leaves me as I force myself not to move. I'm afraid of even breathing at this point because I'm so close to the edge. My body shakes under her, straining under the amount of force it's taking me to do as she told me.

"Such a good boy." She laughs. "You're so obedient."

I shudder at the praise again.

My eyes pop open when she leans over me, her lips pressing against mine. She pulls me into a deep kiss, running her tongue along the seam of my lips before plunging in and tasting every inch of me. I don't hold back while I suck on her tongue, pretending it's one of those perky little nipples instead.

She moans, her pussy squeezing me again.

Fuck, she's really killing me here. Is this some kind of test?

When she parts from our kiss, she smiles at me. "You want to cum, baby?"

I nod quickly, practically breaking my neck to do so.

She laughs and leans back, letting go of my tie. "Okay. Since you've been so obedient, I can let you cum."

For some reason, her words make me grateful. Like I'm happy to have served her so well.

Her hands run up her body again, her hips rolling once more until she's picked up a good pace. My wrists hurt from how hard I tug at the restraints, wanting so badly to get out of them so I can follow the path of her hands with my own.

I moan and let my head fall back onto the pillows, my body so ready to fall over the edge it's ridiculous.

"Come for me," she tells me. "I want to feel you fill me up."

That's all I need to hear before I'm bucking up into her, riding out my orgasm as I spill every last drop into her. She holds her hips up for me, letting me slam up into her a few times before finally collapsing onto the bed again.

I pant, sweat running down my body while my entire world spins on its head.

Fuck, that was so damn hot.

When I roll over, my arms reach out to grab a hold of Emma and pull her close. However, just like last time though, the sheets next to me are cold.

I sigh and slowly peel my eyes open.

I don't know why I expected something different this time around. It isn't like we're anything but a casual fling. But the disappointment hits me harder than I thought it would. Did she not have fun? I paid attention the entire time—made sure of it even—while we were fucking like rabbits.

She seemed completely into it, so what gives?

Sitting up, I rub my hands over my face in frustration. It isn't supposed to be like this, my feelings getting tangled up with what is purely just sex. It isn't like I want to date this girl, although I wouldn't mind. She's a bombshell and can rock it in bed, not to mention she's smart and witty and has an air of mystery surrounding her that intrigues me every time she opens her mouth.

Maybe seeing her again had been a bad idea.

Getting out of bed, I grab my clothes and pull them on, not bothering to shower first. I'll head back to my place, regardless of what time it is. It won't kill me to be late for once in my life, even if I feel like calling off altogether.

I need to pull it together and get this girl out of my mind before I end up tripping and catching feelings for someone I hardly know.

Fuck, am I *that* lonely?

Shaking my head, I slip my watch over my wrist

and head to the bathroom to fix myself before I have to leave. When I flick on the lights, I jump slightly at the red markings covering the mirror. Blinking a few times, I realize that it's words that have been written with what looks like a tube of red lipstick.

It reads: "*Meet me at the bar. 7pm. Don't keep me waiting ;)*"

A grin splits my face.

Oh. This is going to be fun.

CHAPTER 6

Amelia

A PRIVATE CAR picks me up outside of my hotel and takes me to an undisclosed location somewhere along the Hudson River.

When I got the call this morning that the buyer was finally willing to meet me, I had a moment of relief.

Finally things are moving along. The sooner I can get this over with and this deal secured, the faster I can get back home to my mother.

When the car pulls up to a small house a few minutes off of the highway, I lean toward the front and look through the windshield. Next to me, my bodyguard shifts in his seat, readjusting the gun at his hip.

"Miss Amelia, would you like me to wait outside?"

"I'd like you to do a sweep first."

He nods before getting out and coming around my side to open the door for me.

The house is tucked between a bunch of overgrown vegetation and looks long since abandoned. Other than the lone light that shines above the doorway, still on even though it's light outside, I would've thought I'd been dropped off and left to figure out a way back to the city.

Heading up to the house, I hear my bodyguard coming up from behind me and grab me in order to put himself before me as we approach the house. His fist slams against the door a few times, his hand hovering over his gun as we wait for the door to open.

I'm not going home empty handed. Not after running around for weeks trying to get this all sorted out.

When the door opens up, a man stands in the doorway. He has a mean-looking expression on his face that's all business, his eyes giving me a hard once-over. There's a gun strapped to his hip, not even bothering to conceal it from view while eyeing my bodyguard carefully.

"Business?"

I roll my eyes. "Amelia Devlin. I'm expected."

He grunts at me before stepping back from the door to let me in. I don't move; instead, I wait for my bodyguard to step in for me.

"He's taking a sweep," I tell the other man, smirking when he frowns back at me.

He doesn't stop my bodyguard from heading inside and doing a full sweep of the house, coming back with a quick report of no other people inside aside from the one sitting in the living room waiting for me. I nod to him and thank him as he steps outside onto the small porch, keeping his eyes on the other guard.

I brush past the other guard, not bothering to pay him any more attention before heading into the house and down the hallway. I don't have time to play nice and pretend to be grateful for the audience. I have too much shit to do and not enough time in the day to do it.

As I reach the living room, another man stands up from the couch, a book clutched in his hands.

"Amelia, right? Thank you for joining me."

I frown. "...You're not Lavin."

"No, I'm his liaison. He sent me to meet with you first. He doesn't usually agree to meeting anyone before I vet them."

Oh my god, is he serious? "I don't have time to play telephone. Either he gets here within the next half hour or I'm leaving and you can kiss the deal goodbye."

The man holds his hands up, one of them still clutching the book. "Whoa, hold on. Why don't we sit and talk for a bit before you go making that kind of irrational decision?"

My teeth grind together at his words. Irrational? What, because I'm a woman?

God, it's always the same with these mafia families—including my own. They never take women like me seriously, even though I have no problem pulling out my gun and blowing their brains out. It's like they meet a confident and attractive woman and all they see are a pair of tits and a pussy.

I'm so tired of this runaround. I just want to go home to my family.

"You know what?" I turn to leave. "Fuck this and fuck you."

"Miss Devlin, please. Mr. Lavin is only doing this as a precaution. He's unfortunately been experiencing quite a few assassination attempts recently."

That catches my attention.

I look over my shoulder at the man, searching for any kind of hidden agenda or lie in his eyes. He seems to be telling the truth…

Assassination attempts on members of a mafia family aren't unheard of. Hell, it comes with the territory. But it's the amount that has caught my attention. Multiple in the span of a short period of time isn't common and means that you either pissed off the wrong people or you have something valuable everyone wants.

Either way, I'm intrigued.

Turning back around, I walk over and sit down onto the couch across from him. He smiles at me and folds himself back into his own chair, setting the book aside.

"My name is Kenny."

Ugh, I hate the small talk. "Right, so the deal?"

He chuckles at me. "Getting right down to business, I see."

"I'm not one for wasting time."

"I see that." Kenny leans back in his chair, folding one leg over the other. "Mr. Lavin is willing to go through with the deal that was proposed on one condition."

"What?" I bite out.

"He wants forty-five percent of the profit share."

It takes every ounce of effort not to let my mouth fall open. Is this guy *insane*? Not only am I selling him a shitload of product to do whatever he pleases with, but now he wants to profit share? Absolutely fucking not. I don't share profits with anyone, let alone a small fry like Lavin.

I'll admit, I don't know much about the man, and when he contacted me some weeks ago looking to make a deal, I was skeptical. He told me he was new in the business and looking for a long-term relationship as long as the products were good and could be delivered.

Which, in the grand scheme of things, sounds nice. But apparently there were ulterior motives.

"No."

Kenny blinks at me. "No? You don't even consider it?"

"No. I don't do profit shares."

"But your family—"

"The *Devlins* don't do profit shares. He either

takes the deal I'm offering or he can find a new supply chain. I don't care either way. I'll have two clients to replace him with by the end of the day, so his decision on the matter makes no difference to me."

Kenny squirms in his seat, clearly uncomfortable with how upfront I'm being. Sure, it may seem callous, but I don't believe in wasting my breath negotiating. I work on a point-blank system, and if potential buyers don't like it, they can find someone else.

My market would always be saturated with buyers, regardless of how I conduct myself. My family's products are high quality, untraceable, and most of all accessible. A partnership with the Devlins is a partnership for life.

"I'm afraid that I'll need to speak with him before he decides on anything."

I stand. "Whatever. He can come to me then because I'm not doing this again. Either he meets me in person to discuss things or I'm out."

Kenny clears his throat, trying to lighten up the mood but doing anything but. "Well...I'll pass along the message."

Without another word, I head out to the front of the house and step outside to greet my bodyguard, my car still waiting for me in the driveway.

I let myself in and slam the door, glaring at the driver. "Hotel. Now."

CHAPTER 7

Jax

I'M AMPED up by the time I leave the office and head down to the bar.

I don't know what's gotten into me, but Emma's somehow gotten under my skin and into my bloodstream, pumping me full of endorphins every time I think about her. It took me a while to figure out why I'm feeling this way, but I think I've finally nailed exactly why I've latched onto her so quickly.

She's everything I've been missing.

For so long I'd thought about my career and climbing up the ladder, and in my personal life, all of my concerns were with my sister and keeping her safe. But now that she has Johnathan, there is something in my personal life that is lacking.

Which is exactly why Emma's presence crashing into it has been so satisfying.

I doubt she wants any kind of serious relationship,

but that's fine by me. I'm too swamped with work to really focus on having a girlfriend anyways. However, that doesn't also mean I'm not ready to explore whatever it is I have with Emma while she's still here.

She seems kind of stuck on me too, considering she's taken me back to her place twice now and hopefully a third time tonight.

Last night, her appearance had thrown me off a bit, but I recognized her face immediately. Not to mention that alluring charm that practically oozes out of her pores that I can't help but gravitate toward.

Whatever is in store for me tonight, I'm ready for it.

I arrive at the bar a little earlier than we planned for, so I take up a seat at the same table we sat in the night before. I'm a drink and a half in before she finally arrives, looking much different than yesterday and the day before.

Her eyes glaze over me before she heads over to the bar and sits down at one of the stools, waving her hand at the bartender with a bill already in her hand. I watch her closely while she waits for her drink to be made, chatting casually with a couple sitting next to her.

Maybe this is all part of the buildup: making me wait before she comes over and seduces me again. It's kind of fun, I have to admit, not knowing her next move. She's unpredictable in the best way, making this entire thing exciting and nothing like I've ever experienced before.

I wait for her drink to arrive, and when it does, she continues to sit at the bar and sip from it, never once looking back to make sure I'm still sitting at this table waiting for her. I lean forward in my seat.

What is she doing?

Instead of the short bob she was wearing yesterday, today she's sporting a long blond wig that reaches down her back and is curled at the ends. Unlike the other two times I met her, she's wearing a two-piece outfit instead of the tight, form-fitting dresses. It's a longer skirt that hugs her curves with a matching top that rests just below her bra line, showing over her toned stomach.

She looks damn good. Like usual.

And I'm not the only one who notices.

A man down at the end of the bar is eyeing her like a piece of candy, and an irrational type of jealousy comes over me suddenly, surprisingly. By no means does Emma belong to me or owe me anything because we've slept together twice, but I can't help having this sense of protectiveness over her. Like she's mine and anyone who dares to look at her is going to get a punch to the face.

The sudden violence also surprises me. Never once in my entire life have I ever gotten into a physical fight. I didn't exactly believe in that sort of thing and chose to fight my battles in the courtroom instead.

That is how justice is served, after all.

Getting up from my chair, I head over to her and lean against the bar on the side that the man is facing her from to completely block his view of her. Her eyes flick over to me, running up and down my chest before focusing on my face.

"Oh, hello."

"Hi." Now that I can see her more up close, I notice she's wearing a completely different style of makeup than yesterday too. "You look really good tonight."

She smiles. "Really? You think so?"

I grin at her. "Oh, I know so."

She laughs and sips her drink, watching me closely. The pucker of her lips pulls me in, tempting me to lean over and swoop her into a heated kiss. I can already feel my body responding to her. She's definitely a magnet, and I'm the one circling around her orbit.

"I'm Maxine." She smiles again.

That...has me blinking. "...Maxine?"

She nods. "And you?"

I narrow my eyes at her. What the hell is happening? Is this like a roleplaying sort of deal?

Not that I'm opposed to it, but I wish I'd been in on the game because I would've come back here dressed up as someone new too.

"I'm, uh...Jax."

"Jax." She nods, setting her drink down. "It's nice to meet you."

Her tone is much more friendly than the last two times we spoke to each other. Before she had a sultry nature to her that bordered on mysterious and alluring. But now she seems much more open and honest, like she wants me to flirt with her and seduce *her* back to her hotel room.

Leaning back, I sink onto the stool behind me, making sure to keep blocking that guy from earlier. "Yeah. You come around here often?"

Something flashes in her eyes, and a small smirk tugs at her lips. Ah, so this is a game. I must be playing into it well because she leans forward toward me until I'm able to clearly see down her shirt.

"I'm new in town. You live around here?"

I'm practically breathless as I say, "I'm from up town."

"That's fancy over there, I here."

"Oh." I wave my hand. "It's nothing special. You here on business, or…?"

There's a deviousness to her smile. "Something like that."

I felt closer to getting to know her when she told me her name was Emma. But now that she's told me her name is Maxine, I realize I don't know her at all, and it's killing me. God, I want to know more about her so badly. Do I ask, or is this all part of the game? She must be a part of some kink club and her "business" is scooping out new people to bring back to her place. Honestly, I'm totally into it. Even if it's kind of wild and like nothing I've ever done before.

"Well, Maxine." I reach forward and tuck a piece of her hair behind her ear. By this time I know the drill. "What do you say we get out of here?"

Her smile widens. "I'd love that."

CHAPTER 8

Jax

I'M NOT surprised when morning comes and I find the hotel room completely empty. At this point, I'm rolling with the punches and letting myself enjoy the ride while I have it.

Getting out of bed, I head to the bathroom and find what appears to be a black business card sitting on the edge of the sink. When I grab it, it's surprisingly heavy. That's when I notice that it's not made of paper, but of metal. Rotating it in my hand, I spot a signature on the back of it that reads: *A. Devlin* along with a phone number.

A. Devlin? I wonder what that means.

Excitement hits me, though. Is she actually giving me her phone number to contact her?

Fuck, I hope so. I want to keep doing this for as long as I can. Emma, Maxine, or whoever she is—my mystery girl—is a woman like no other. She brings out a wild side in me that I never knew existed. Not to mention all of the new things she's been showing me.

Who knew sex like this could be so fun?

Heading over to my clothes that are still strewn about the room, I grab my pants and shake out my phone. My fingers are quick to unlock the screen and start a new contact, one that I label appropriately as "mystery girl."

I hope one day she tells me her real name, but the anonymity of this all is fun too. Should I come up with an alter ego too? Or is that taking away from her fun too much?

Hm…I'll have to think about it. I don't know the first thing about roleplay.

I send a text over to the number, a quick *"hey it's Jax"* before tossing my phone onto the bed and dressing once again. I tuck the business card into my pocket, keeping it just in case I need it later for something—which is a strange thought but who's ever seen a metal business card before?

Not me, at least.

I hear my phone go off and grab it, checking to see if I've been answered. The number that I texted has sent over only an address and no other message attached. I click on it and bring up my maps app.

Judging by the block, I had a fair guess that it's somewhere on the upper east side. She probably got a new hotel, seeing as how she'd taken me back to this one three times now.

A sudden thought hits me.

Wait...what if she's running from someone? Or cheating on her spouse?

I frown and lower my phone. Did I...care?

I'm not sure. I've never been the "other man" or whatever it's called, so I have no idea how to handle that if that came to be the case. Not to mention if her spouse did find out, would they come around to beat me for stealing their woman?

"Shit," I mumble to myself.

This would be about the time my sister would be yelling at me for being so careless and stupid. She'd have a field day if she knew I've been sleeping with some random woman I met at a bar who was into roleplay and didn't tell me anything about herself other than she liked to dominate me in bed and punish me for disobeying her orders.

What the hell would Kylie even say to that, anyway? Finding out for myself that I was into that kind of thing was weird enough, but for my sister to know too?

No thanks, I'll pass.

I check my phone again, seeing that no other text has come in other than the address. I'm a little disheartened, but I'm sure she's out busy doing something important. She always seems to leave early, so that's an indication that she either has an early-start job or she's rushing back home before her husband catches her out.

Ugh...I really hope it's not the latter.

Though, knowing my luck, it will be.

Shoving my phone back into my pocket, I head out of the hotel to try and get my mind back in order before heading to work. Either way, I'm going to the location on the note. And it if so happens to be a setup, then so be it.

At least I had a few great lays before I got buried six feet under by an angry husband.

IT TURNS out that the address Emma/Maxine had given me was to a *very* fancy restaurant in upper Manhattan. I'd only been here once, and it was when Kylie and I had taken a nightly walk and had seen how packed the place was.

We'd gotten curious and had wandered inside, only to be shown the door soon after and told not to come back without the proper attire.

It had been the first time in both of our lives where privilege had smacked us right in the face unapologetically.

By no means are either of us poor now, but damn...that event sure showed us otherwise.

While at work today, I'd barely gotten through two case files before I'd gotten distracted doing a deep dive on the restaurant as well as trying to reverse look-up the phone number Emma/Maxine had given me.

I'd come up with absolutely nothing and had heard nothing back from her at all in regards to my text. I'd been tempted a few times to double text her, but I felt like that would be coming across as too needy. This—whatever we had—that is slowly building between us feels like it's still hanging on by a delicate thread.

I'm not going to let anything in my irrational brain spoil it right when it's really starting to get good.

After parking my car and walking the block down to the restaurant, I realize right as I'm heading inside that I have absolutely no idea what our reservation is under. Would it be my name or whatever one she's decided to go with today?

Shit, I didn't think this through.

Shoving my hands into my pockets, I try to step past the hostess stand to see into the restaurant, but it's at such an awkward angle that I can barely see anything.

"Can I have the name for your reservation, sir?"

I glance back to the hostess. "Uh…it might be under Jax."

In my head, I'm crossing my fingers. The hostess scans her list, frowning as she reaches the bottom of it. "I don't see that name on here. What's your last name?"

Shit.

Stepping around her again, I try and peer back into the restaurant once more.

"Sir?"

I catch the sight of a bombshell brunette over at the bar, and my heart soars.

That has to be her.

"Sir—"

"Sorry, I just saw my date." I point past her. "Can I go over?"

She gives me a wary look. "Uh…"

Without waiting for her to answer me, I dart past her and head over to the bar. If I'm wrong, this is going to be totally embarrassing, but at this point I'm too juiced up to really care. I've been waiting all day to see her and have been craving the taste of her like she's water in the middle of a desert.

As I get closer to her, I noticed that she has her phone pressed to her ear and she's turning away from the rest of the restaurant. She's talking in a quiet voice with one of her fingers dug into her opposite ear to block out some of the noise from the restaurant.

I sit on the stool next to her, waving my hand at the bartender, who nods at me to let me know he'll be with me soon.

"Mmm…okay. Thank you, you too…" she says quietly before taking the phone away from her ear.

As she lowers it, she stares at the screen for a long moment. There's a picture on the top of the contact, but from here, I can't tell who it is.

Oh fuck, what if it's her husband?

Shit.

She sighs softly before shaking her head and straightening up. Her phone is quickly shoved into her purse before it's snapped shut once more.

As she turns to me, I straighten my shoulders. Ready for the game to begin.

CHAPTER 9

Amelia

When I arrive at the bar, I take a seat near the end where I know I'll get the least amount of attention. It isn't every day that I find myself dedicating my time to one man, but so far Jax has been an outstanding lay.

I can't help but let my thoughts drift to him during the day, even when I'm elbow-deep in figuring out this deal with Lavin. My mind tends to wander to sex when I'm stressed, and it's been a hell of a stressful week.

He's been an excellent distraction from my frustrations the past few days, and I can't help but wonder is it that? A simple distraction? Or is he slowly starting to wiggle his way into my life unexpectedly? I shudder at the thought. I don't have time for a relationship—it's unrealistic considering I'm needed back home in Ireland the moment this deal is done, but for some stupid reason, my heart wants to entertain the thought.

It's not that I think Jax would be a bad pick, but he would definitely not be able to keep up with my lifestyle. Other than the sex, we are like polar opposites. I play hard and fast, dirty money and even dirtier deals exchanging from my hands quicker than it takes for some people to breathe. I've lived my entire life in a position that grants me as much freedom as I'm willing to take a bullet for. Then there are those like Jax who find comfort in a mundane life.

He wears simple but expensive suits, which indicates his job requires conservative authority. Despite his good looks and chiseled body, nothing about his presence or energy screams, "Look at me."

Jax is more straightlaced and uptight, someone you'd take home to meet your mother. Not my mother. She's a different kind of breed. Bred to lead a very dangerous pack from birth. She would chew him up and spit him to the wolves that follow her and let them clean up the scraps. He's in no way prepared for a Devlin family introduction.

As soon as a martini is sat down in front of me, I nod to the bartender and take a sip from it. The cool burn races down my throat, settling my frayed nerves from earlier. I hadn't expected to walk away from that deal feeling as frustrated as I did, but Kenny somehow knew how to push every one of my buttons.

In my lap, I feel my purse vibrating with a phone call. It makes me sigh and set down my drink. Speak of the damn devil...it's probably Kenny calling to bother me about another offer. Unless he has something worth my time—no profit sharing and forking over my damn money—I already know how annoyed I'm going to be at the end of this phone call.

I pull my phone out of my purse, not bothering to look at the caller ID before putting it up to my ear. "What?"

There's a soft laugh on the other end. "Hi, love, sounds like you've had a rough day?"

I blink a few times in surprise. "...Mom?"

Her laughter turns into a haggard cough. My heart squeezes while she wheezes, her tired lungs sounding strained under the efforts of simply breathing too hard. All of a sudden, I feel my eyes start to burn and quickly look up at the lights beaming over me and blink a few times before any tears fall.

"How are you, my sweet?" she finally asks after getting her coughing under control.

"Um...fine. How...how are you?"

I already know the answer before the awkward question is tumbling out of me. It's a polite enough question, but we both know what her real answer is, even if she won't tell me. Sean, her caretaker, has been giving me day-by-day updates on her condition, and each one of them is worse than the last.

I know my mother doesn't have much time left

on this earth, hence why I'm trying so damn hard to get this fucking deal done and over with. I never would have come if she hadn't asked me herself. She told me to get the deal handled so she can rest peacefully. As frail as she may sound, Fiona Devlin is one woman few people dare cross, and they definitely don't refuse a request when asked to handle business for her.

This deal is the last loose end I need to tie up before I can return back to our family and take care of my mother until she eventually succumbs to her sickness.

And I'm terrified it won't be much longer before that day comes; my heart constricts painfully just thinking about it. I can't stand that thought of having to bury my mother or saying goodbye to her. None of what is in my future am I prepared for.

But I don't have a choice. We all die eventually.

"I'm all right, my love. I wanted to call," I can hear her heave in a deep breath, "and ask you how you've been. Sean tells me you're still working on that deal."

My shoulders hunch forward as my body tries to hold itself together. I can't cry, not while I'm on the phone with her. All I want to do is tell Lavin to fuck off and leave this deal unfinished in order to go home and be with my family whom I know need me. But I know she's counting on me. Not to mention the consequences could lead to worse things than me missing precious time with my mother, as fucked up as that sounds.

I can't afford him getting angry and retaliating against me or my family right now. We're not vulnerable by any means, but I need everyone's attention focused inward and not to our enemies on the outside.

We'll need all the strength we can get once my mother passes—especially with her passing on her title to me afterward. Ireland is still quite traditional when it comes to women leading the family. Many will oppose it, as they did with my mother when she took the title from her father, but as long as the Devlins all stand together, we'll knock whoever the fuck we need to down.

"Yeah, just negotiating the details and then I'll be home."

"Good." I can tell she's smiling by how warm her tone is. "How are the American men over there treating you?"

I hold back a sigh. She's fishing, of course, about my love life. She's been doing this ever since I left a few months ago to embark on this godforsaken endeavor and hasn't let up since. I think it's her way of making sure I'll have someone when she's not around anymore, which sure, is a sweet thought, but even entertaining the thought makes my throat feel raw from holding back my tears. She always wanted me with someone who has strong Irish bloodlines, but I think she'd settle for any male who could handle me at this point.

Even when I was growing up, I never really

imagined my life without my mother around. She'd been a constant figure from the time I was born, through my dad and brother passing, and till now. There was never a time when I *didn't* have her. So what am I going to do when she's gone?

Fuck... Now the tears are really starting to come.

I fucking hate this.

"Amelia?" Her voice is soft.

"Fine." I clear my throat, trying to calm down. "Most of them, anyway."

"Well, I know you can handle yourself. I hope to see you soon, love."

I clear my throat again. The hope in her voice guts me. "You taking all your meds and vitamins? Has Sean taken you out to walk recently to get some fresh air?"

She laughs again. "Yes, I'm being well taken care of. Stop worrying about me. You've got business to take care of."

Her voice completely changes when she's talking about business. Such strength and passion has led her to accomplish so much throughout her reign, and that makes me smile. I swear that passion is what's kept her alive for the past few years. I admire her so much... "Mom, I miss you."

"I miss you too, my sweet flower. I love you."

"I love you too."

"You take care of yourself, okay? I'll check in tomorrow."

"Mmm...okay." I gulp down another bout of tears

that threatens to spill down my cheeks. Fuck, I hate being so far away from her like this. "Thank you, you too…"

"Goodbye, my love."

I slowly pull the phone away from my ear and stare down at the screen as my mother's contact slowly fades. Her picture is of the two of us when we visited the UK two years ago on a business trip, before she got really sick. We're both smiling wide into the camera and in the background is that famous Ferris wheel that right now I can't remember the name of for the life of me.

It's one of my favorite pictures because you can see her strength and the life in her eyes, the youthfulness in her full cheeks—all before the cancer sucked every last bit of light and joy from her body. I run my thumb over the screen when it darkens, my own reflection staring back at me—forlorn and miserable.

"Hey." I jump slightly at the sound of a familiar voice and turn to stare at Jax.

Fuck, I completely forgot about our little rendezvous. I hold back another sigh and instead tuck a piece of my wig's hair behind my ear. After my phone call, I'm absolutely not in the mood at all anymore. Any sense of horniness I had brewing in me earlier is now completely extinguished.

He smiles at me in that crooked way of his and leans his body against the side of the bar. One of his arms is propped up on the counter, and he's completely facing me, ignoring the rest of the restaurant as well as the bartender looking over at us curiously. He acts like I'm the center of his world when he looks at me like that.

For some reason that makes me…nervous.

I shake off the feeling and slide on a devious smirk that I hope doesn't look too fake. "Hello there, stranger."

Something in his eyes shifts, and it has him tilting his head curiously at me. He glances down at the phone still clutched in my hand before bouncing his eyes back up to mine. "Everything okay?"

My lips part slightly in surprise, but other than that, I keep my face neutral. How does he know something's wrong? I know for a fact I'm not obvious when it comes to any of my emotions, except for anger—*that* I have a hard time hiding when someone pisses me off.

I pride myself in being hard for people to read, especially when it comes to being open and vulnerable like I feel right now. Speaking with my mother always has me feeling raw, especially with us being so far away from each other.

There's no telling how long I have left with her, and the more time I waste being in this stupid country, the worse her death is going to hit me when it comes. I already know I'm going to be a complete and utter mess, and that's without the guilt of not being able to spend what little days she has left *with* her.

"I'm not sure I know what you mean?" I say and lean back a little, letting the deep V of my dress do all the talking for me.

For some reason, Jax doesn't even glance down at my exposed tits though.

"You sure? You seem…upset."

I glare at him. Does he think this is deeper than it is? He needs to know his lane and stay the fuck out of my personal life. "I'm sorry, who the hell are you?"

That has him immediately backing up and putting his hands up in defense. "I-I'm sorry, I didn't mean—"

Pushing myself off of the stool, I stand and collect my bag. I hardly touched my martini at all, but I throw down a few bills to cover my tab. I'd been planning on racking up Jax's before dragging him back to my hotel room, but now I'm too pissed off to even think about handcuffing him to my bed.

Maybe this is my way of punishing us both. We need distance; this is all getting too cozy for me. I don't know what I was thinking.

"W-Wait," he calls out as I walk away from him.

I don't stop though and continue through the restaurant and out the door. Honestly? Fuck him. Who does he think he is? And also: what the hell does he think he *knows* about me? Telling me I look upset… What a fucking idiot!

I'm fuming by the time I get out onto the street and tap at my phone to order an Uber back to my hotel. This has been a complete waste of time. Why I even bothered to entertain whatever the hell Jax and I had been doing was stupid of me. I let my own vices win against me, and now I'm paying for it by that embarrassing display.

Actually, he's lucky I didn't pull out the Glock I have tucked inside of my purse—

"Emma, wait," he calls from behind me.

I groan to myself. Of course he can't take a fucking hint.

Whipping around, I glare at him. "Go away."

He frowns, stopping short. "Look, I'm sorry. I didn't mean—"

"What?" I snap at him. "What is it you think we are doing here?"

He blinks, putting his hands up. "I don't know, I—"

"You don't?" Now my anger is really heating up. I step forward and jab my finger into his chest a few times. "You're a good fuck, or did you forget that? We're not in a relationship. It's a way for me to relieve stress and have some fun. It's not a therapy session. You don't want to fuck your therapist, Jax!"

He flinches at my words but strangely enough, but he doesn't back up or run away. Instead, he stands there and takes it.

Why? Why doesn't he just leave and go find some other girl to bring back to his place for a fuck?

"I'm sorry, Emma. I don't want to be your therapist. It just seemed to me that your phone call upset you, and I wanted to make sure you were okay before we… I don't know. Did our usual…" He waves his hand around.

The genuine concern in his eyes has me reeling back from him. What the hell is this? Is he serious?

I bark out a laugh. "Don't tell me you've gotten attached. You do know you're just a play thing for me, right? That's all this is. It's a game."

This time, my words don't look like they faze him at all, despite how cruel my tone is. "I understand, but I'm also not a robot. I do have feelings. I may mean nothing to you, but it also doesn't feel right to take advantage of you when you're vulnerable."

For some reason, that amuses me. "Take advantage of me? Honey, you couldn't even if you tried. Trust me, I'm *much* scarier than I look."

The way his eyes crinkle at the corners has me wanting to back up away from him even more. He's looking at me with such…affection that it's really starting to freak me out. "Oh, I'm aware. I have no doubt about that."

My jaw clicks as I clench my teeth together. Men are so fucking annoying. Why does he think he sees something he doesn't? Vulnerability. Ha! I really don't need this shit right now.

You know what? Fuck him. I'm over this.

Turning away from him, I head down the street, my heels clicking loudly. I don't have time to stand around and wait for my Uber to get here while Jax continues to try and talk to me. I can't stand listening to him for another second or else I really might give into my desires and blow a hole through his fucking abdomen for pissing me off.

"Wait—Emma."

I feel a hand wrap around my arm and stop me from walking any further. Without even thinking about it, I turn and jut my knee out, catching him right between the legs with a hard jab. Shit! I didn't even mean to do it; it was an instinctual self-defense technique. One I've used many times before. He chokes out a groan before crumbling to the ground, clutching his bruised balls between his legs. Even if it was a triggered response, I can't lie; I am a little happy to be in charge of my emotions again.

"F-Fuck...!"

I stand over him, a satisfied smirk washing over my face. "See, here's the thing: you don't know the first thing about me. If I wanted to, Jax, I would absolutely terrify you. Are you understanding me?"

I fist my hands in the back of his hair, yanking his head back so he's looking up at me. "You're lucky that the worst thing I did to you was handcuff you to my bed. Not for a second did you think I could've done far worse to you while you were that vulnerable. For all you knew, I could've robbed you blind, and you're too much of an idiot to realize that."

His eyes widen at me. "Well, actually that thought did cross my mind—"

"Then why in God's name did you let it go that

far?" I spit out and let go of his hair. "Jesus, Jax, you really got to be more careful."

Stepping away from him, I readjust my clutch under my arm and turn to walk away from him again. I don't get more than two feet before he's calling out to me again.

"Emma…!" His voice is choked. "Please…don't go. I know what it is. I mean what we have, and I don't care!"

That had me stopping in my tracks. I turn to look over my shoulder at him, my eyes narrowing. "About. What."

He's bent over the sidewalk with one hand flush against it to balance his weight while the other still holds his balls. His face is slightly red, but from what, I'm not sure. Maybe the kick to the balls or him yelling at me, who knows? His eyes are wide and vulnerable, a combination that makes my heart stutter for some reason.

"I know it's all a game to you." He heaves in a breath. "I know you're terrifying. But for the first time in a long time, I feel alive again. It makes me want you in my life no matter what the role is…"

…I don't believe him.

In fact, I can see something he can't. He's lying to himself; he wants more.

"You…" The words are slow to churn inside of my brain, working overtime to understand the double meaning behind them. "…Want me in your life." Clearly he really doesn't know what he's getting himself into.

He chuckles lightly. "Weirdly enough, something tells me I should be scared of you, terrified even, but I'm not. I'm drawn to you. And not just because you're hot, and we've had the best sex I've ever had, but there's something about you. Your energy, who you are, that's what I'm wildly attracted to."

Who the hell is this man?

My fingers rub together at my thigh as I readjust my weight slightly to turn a little more to face him. "I really don't want to hurt you."

"Now you're thinking I'm too fragile. Don't worry about me. I know I'm playing with fire here. I'm well aware," comes his easy reply.

And just like that, he completely accepts the truth I'm giving him without even knowing how deep it runs. I can't decide if he's actually a complete idiot or he's the most persistent man I've ever met.

Maybe a bit of both?

Either way, it has me shaking my head. Though my anger is slowly subsiding. Walking back over to him, I assess him carefully. He doesn't...seem to be lying to me. Though, even if he is, what would be his motive? I know for a fact he isn't working for any of my enemies. One: because he'd be way too obvious, and two: I can tell there isn't a mean bone in his body.

People like me, like those in this business, we always have a certain look in our eyes that's a dead giveaway. It's a look that tells you, "Yeah, I've killed," or, "Yeah, I've done some shady shit that you're going to regret asking about," and Jax has neither of those.

His eyes are filled with honesty and warmth that I'm not used to seeing—almost like he *likes* looking at me, that whatever he sees excites him.

What those things are could be anyone's guess.

Sighing at him, I rest my hand on my hip. "Can you stand?"

He looks down at himself. "Probably."

I roll my eyes and offer him a hand. "Come on."

When he takes it, I haul him back up onto his feet.

"You better not make me regret this," I tell him before pulling out my phone again and ordering an Uber.

My stomach does a weird flip when he smiles and says with confidence, "Not a chance."

CHAPTER 10

Amelia

"How are your balls?" I ask, crossing my arms while standing in front of him.

Jax sits back on my bed, leaning against the frame while a hand towel filled with fresh ice from the machine down the hall rests on his lap. He snorts at me, looking me over with a hungry look in his eyes despite his very obviously bruised dick.

"It's a little sore."

"Mhmm." I give him a disbelieving look, knowing how hard my knee jabbed into him and how quickly he went down.

Honestly, why are guys always so prideful? There's no shame in admitting when you've been bested. Especially from a woman like me. Sometimes it feels great when I'm underestimated because the satisfaction from seeing another man's face when I've beaten them is enough to make up for the anger that they caused doubting me in the first place.

But with situations like this, it kind of just feels like I'm kicking a puppy.

Jax must be completely delusional; even after kicking him in the balls, he still wants to be around me. That's the only explanation I have.

"What about you?" he asks.

That has me raising a brow. "What *about* me?"

"How are you?" He lets his words trail off.

I sigh again. Of course even after getting kicked in the balls for the same subject, he is treading on thin ice. Maybe he really is delusional after all. Suffice to say that I've somehow gotten a hold of a crazy one…even if he is good in bed.

"Did you forget you're not my therapist?"

He leans forward slightly, narrowing his eyes. "Okay, fair. So just pretend I'm a stranger. One you can vent to. That's accurate right?"

Oh my god, is he serious?

"You keep digging your grave deeper."

He smiles at me. "No grave, just a stranger."

"Why?"

It's an obvious challenge, a way for me to distance myself from him even though I doubt he'll rise to it and defend himself. Typically when I challenge a man, they double back and pretend that they never cared at all. It's always some kind of ego trip for them until I poke at the right buttons and get them to realize that they've overstayed their welcome.

See, here's the thing: I only let people get away

with as much as I *want* them to. There's no illusion to it that speaks differently, and the only reason I allow things like that to happen is because sometimes I'm feeling a little chaotic and like to see where it goes.

Hence, why I can play around with men's feelings without feeling bad.

Except, when they start crossing over into the territory of *caring*…that is when I have to put my foot down. Make no mistake, there won't be any entanglement of feelings from my end, and I most certainly am not going to entertain any from his end either.

I'm not looking to get myself lost in some romance that threatens to sweep me off my feet and carry me away into some godforsaken sunset. I live in the real world where love is a fucking delusion made up by people who are too bored with their own lives that they need to invade someone else's.

"You sure are making things complicated," he throws back at me.

"Because that's stupid. We don't know each other."

Jax grins suddenly. "Exactly. That's why it shouldn't be complicated. Strangers…with no feelings and no attachment."

I stare at him. What exactly is happening here? Did he just flip things around on me?

"Oh, come on, Emma," he says amusingly. "It's

your last chance. I'm not gonna ask again. Don't you ever want to confess who you really are to a total stranger who won't judge you and who you will probably never see again?"

Jesus, he seems to be oddly good at this game. I can't lie, the thought is appealing. "Why? Why should I do that?" I snap back, daring him to call me out.

He huffs at me. "Because it feels good to let your demons see the light, to not hold them inside any longer. I promise, it won't make you less dangerous."

"I'm not sure about that."

He throws me another amused look filled with warmth and fondness. I hate it. "Come on, there's something freeing about embracing your demons. Exciting even."

"What, is the fucking getting too boring for you?"

"Not at all." He laughs. "I feel like I embraced some of my own demons when we met. You pulled them out of me. It's that line you want to cross but don't think you can because you'll be judged. Even if people don't know those things about you, you can't help feel like they do."

"Why would you do that?"

He shrugs a shoulder and readjusts the ice on his lap. "I don't know. I was drawn to you like flame to a fire. I could feel the fire inside you. My flame has been dwindling away for too long. I just didn't know what to do about it. When we came together, it made me want to be in touch with a side of myself I've denied for many years. And I'm starting to realize I like that side of myself. But I've had to hide it from everyone so as not to disappoint them. Do you understand what I'm saying?"

My arms slowly unfold from across my chest to drop down on either side of me. I…hate to admit it, but I kind of do. Not in the sense of me wanting to suddenly let my guard down and let him see the deepest parts of me. But…the way Jax speaks does make me want to know why he ticks the way he does.

He's flipped it around on me again. The more he's talking, I'm becoming increasingly curious about who he is. But as they say, curiosity does kill the cat. However, with all of this curiosity flying around, I am starting to wonder which one of us is the cat?

"Yeah…I get it," I finally say.

Even without him knowing my past, I'm sure he's come to the conclusion by now that my bark isn't as bad as my bite. Contrary, my bite is something that most people run screaming from. I'm not one to be messed with, especially when I'm faced with the decision of me or them. I have a family to protect, and like hell I'm sacrificing myself for some asshole who can barely keep their head on straight.

He brightens up at my words. "We don't have to be friends, Emma."

I sigh. "Amelia."

"What?"

I can't believe I'm doing this.

But...what the hell? It's not like I'm ever going to see him again after this.

"My name," I say again, "is Amelia."

CHAPTER 11

Jax

I CAN'T BELIEVE what I'm hearing.

"Amelia..." I try the name on my tongue, taste it between my lips.

I want to whisper and yell it all at the same time.

Amelia.

I can't help but wonder if this is really her name this time. But honestly, Amelia suits her. Emma always seemed like such a stretch when I thought of her with that name; it was far too innocent sounding to match the vibrant woman in front of me, and Maxine seemed a little too coy. Like she was hiding behind a mask that made her more alluring rather than the dangerous minx that is standing before me.

Whatever kind of buzz is running through my veins right now that's making me feel high due to her telling me her actual name is something I wish I could bottle up and keep for the rest of my life. I've never felt a thrill like this before, other than when I'm strapped to her bed fucking her.

I want to know everything about Amelia—everything she'll let me know, at least. She has secrets, that much is obvious, but what exactly are they?

She doesn't strike me as the type to get herself into unnecessary trouble, but that doesn't mean it doesn't find her. There's a difference between seeking a fight and finding one, and it seems to me that she fits that latter of the two.

My eyes track her when she moves over to me and the bed, sinking down onto it by my feet while still maintaining some sort of distance between us. Whatever she's wary about makes me a little sad—like she's expecting me to use whatever she says against her. I can't help but wonder who in her life has hurt her so badly for her to have such a hard time trusting people's intentions.

I'm not ignorant in knowing that even though we've hooked up, I'm still a stranger to her. Of course I know that. But for this level of scrutiny to come from her, it must mean that whoever betrayed her in the past, or whatever loss she's suffered, has cost her greatly.

"I don't get you, Jax." She sighs again. "Why do you care to know me? I thought we were having fun."

"Of course we are," I answer automatically. "I'm just giving you the opportunity to feel what I feel.

Remember? Freeing the demons and all that? It does sound a little appealing, doesn't it?"

At least my lawyer skills have finally come in handy outside of work. Adjusting my approach with Amelia has seemed to soften her aggression a little. At work I'm always the guy they send it to flip the script on someone without them being able to see it coming. Once that happens, they end up spilling details near and dear to their heart without even realizing why they are doing it.

The fact that she thinks she's the only one with a dangerous skill set makes me smile to myself. Hers is more of an "in your face" kind of thing, but with me, no one sees it coming until it's too late.

Maybe she should be more afraid of me than she realizes.

"You're a different kind of man, Jax."

I laugh a little. "Really? What makes you say that?"

She rolls her eyes, but there's a playful touch to her smile as she says, "You trying to cuddle me after falling asleep in my bed after I fucked you."

I wince. "Oh...guilty."

"Letting a stranger handcuff you to a bed," she continues.

There's a different kind of intimacy that comes from letting yourself be completely vulnerable to another person while having sex. I had no control whatsoever, so I had to trust Amelia without even knowing her.

And yet, all she'd done was rock my fucking world.

"Let's just say that's not my usual style, but you are something different entirely."

She gives me a curious look. "Maybe I should be asking who you are...*Jax*."

She eyes me up and down for a long moment, something passing in her eyes before coming to some conclusion in her head. I don't move, even going so far as to hold my breath when she slides back further onto the bed and crawls over to me.

My body heats instantly despite the cold compress resting in my lap. Even though my cock's still a little sore, I can already feel it responding to Amelia the closer she gets to me. Her hands grab onto my knees and press them down against the bed while she crawls between them.

She's looking at me with a hunger that I know I'm more than reciprocating in my own gaze. I want her so badly that I'd do anything. Whatever she wants, I'll give it to her, no questions asked.

"How's your dick feeling?" she murmurs to me, digging her nails into my knees.

I toss the washcloth of ice immediately. "Fine."

She laughs at that. "Oh really. You're not going to cry when I start bouncing on it?"

Her words have me swallowing down a groan. "All good here."

"Hmmm." Her hands move from my knees up to

my inner thighs, squeezing as she goes. "I guess I'll have to test that out, huh?"

Fuck, I'm so ready for this.

The first thing she does is test how sore I am by grabbing me over my pants. I'm already hard under her hand, even though the area is still numb to the touch. I can tell that as soon as she puts her hands on me, though, that I'm going to light up like fire.

Before I know it, Amelia is unzipping my pants and tugging me out of them, my cock springing free as it stands at half-mast. I have to say, I'm a little impressed with myself. Despite the cold from the ice, I'm still raring to go.

It also helps that a fucking bombshell is in front of me, wrapping her hand around the base of my cock, though.

Groaning, I lean back and let her touch me. She expertly strokes me a few times, the numbness from the ice finally wearing off as her hand warms me up again. I throw an arm over my eyes, letting her do whatever the fuck she wants to me. At this point, if she wanted to do something wild like acupuncture while she fucked me, I'd probably let her.

"Jax," she says, gripping me tight. "You're so happy to see me."

"Usually am," I grunt, lifting my arm up slightly to look at her.

She smirks down at me before leaning forward, those cherry red lips of hers wrapping around the head of my cock as she swallows me into her hot, wet mouth.

"Ohhh fuck..."

Her tongue teases me as she rolls it around the back of my shaft. She keeps her hand gripping the base while her cheeks hollow out to form a suction around my already leaking head. It feels so fucking good, but I want more. I always do when it comes to her. I want her to swallow me whole and choke on it.

Letting my horny brain get the better of me, I reach over and thread my fingers into her hair. The wig she's wearing is stiff to the touch, so it makes it hard to grip onto anything without actually ripping it right off her head.

Before I can do any of that, though, she pops her mouth off of me and slaps my hand away. "Naughty, who said you can control this?"

Oh shit.

Letting me go completely, Amelia leans to put a hand on my chest in order to reach over me and grab the handcuffs still chained to the back of the headboard.

"Since you think the ball's in your court, let me remind you that it's not."

She grabs one of my arms and yanks it up, cuffing me before I have a chance to yank it out of her grip. Not that I actually would but her punishing me is the sexiest thing I think I've ever experienced.

Fuck, I'm so done for with her.

As she clips the cuff around my other wrist, she

leans back, satisfied. "Much better. I like this look on you."

I have to laugh. "What, me at your mercy?"

She smirks. "Exactly."

Sliding back down to where she was between my legs, she grips my cock again and leans over it. A line of spit leaves her mouth and dribbles onto the head, wetting it and trailing down to where she catches it with her hand again as she strokes upward.

Her thumb rolls around the head a few times, causing my hips to jerk with each swipe.

"So eager," she tells me. "You want me to fuck you that badly, huh?"

"What can I say?" My voice sounds strained, even to my ears. "I've been waiting for you."

"How sweet."

When she hikes up her dress, I unconsciously tug at my restraints. Maybe it's a good thing she put me in these because all I want to do is grab her and roll her over until she's under me and drive my cock down inside of her—fucking her into oblivion.

Amelia soon straddles me and lifts her hips up just enough to get the tip of my cock pressing against her hole. She slides down onto me slowly, almost in an agonizing way that makes me want to thrust up into her and finally get her seated all the way onto it.

I hold back though. As much as my brain is telling me to do that—to try and take over—I resist.

Because the truth of it is that I like this just as much as she does.

"You going to be good for me?" She bites her lip as she sits all the way down on me.

I nod quickly. Fuck, I'll be whatever she wants me to be.

She rides me, her hands steady on my lower belly as she holds herself up. Her hips move along me, gliding my cock in and out of her in the perfect way that has my toes curling as I try and hold myself back from cumming already.

She looks so fucking good up there with her tits bouncing and her body arched back as she enjoys fucking me. I don't care if this is her using me for her own benefit, because if this is the view I get from it, I'm all in.

"Mmmm, so good," she moans, her head tilting back while her eyes close.

She lets herself go, riding me until her body shakes with an orgasm and her thighs slap around my hips. Her pussy grips mine, pulsating around me while I choke out a groan and cum inside of her.

My balls squeeze, emptying everything they have into her as she continues to ride me through it. Finally she slows, her body coming to a stop while she stares down at me.

Holy shit...

When she leans over to uncuff me, my arms fall on either side of my bed, my breath punching out of me. It has Amelia laughing softly at me and then falling over onto the bed next to me.

I pant and stare up at the ceiling.

Holy shit…

Next to me, Amelia relaxes and hums as she curls up onto her side. "Now *that* was a good fuck."

My head turns to look at her, heart still pounding heavy in my chest. She looks absolutely stunning with her sweat-slicked skin glistening in the dim lighting from the light over by the door. The fibers of her wig slightly stick to her skin but give her that sexed-out look that drives me wild.

She has a small smile tugging at her lips, and those beautiful eyes of hers are closed, letting her long lashes fan over her cheekbones.

All in all, she is stunning.

My heart stutters in my chest again when she lets out a content sigh.

Fuck, I'm so screwed.

CHAPTER 12

Jax

WHEN I WAKE UP, I already know what to expect.

Cracking my eyes open, I wince at the light coming through the uncovered windows next to the bed. Groaning to myself, I slowly sit up and rub my hands over my eyes, scrubbing the sleep from them before slowly blinking them open once again.

The room looks the same as it always does—Amelia's belongings lay scattered everywhere, but she's nowhere to be found.

I don't know why I try to get my hopes up every time this happens, but I never fail to disappoint myself in the process. There's most likely another message waiting for me in the bathroom, but for some reason, that doesn't quite satisfy me this time. Of course, the thrill is always enticing, but I'd been hoping that she would've stuck around after our talk last night.

Well, I guess it wasn't really a *talk* so much as an *understanding.*

Still, what the hell did a guy have to do to keep a woman from skipping out on him every morning? We'd been sleeping together almost the entire week; is it really that much to ask for a morning together eating breakfast?

Shaking my head, I pull myself out of the sheets and off the bed. I might as well take a shower before I head over to my place and change. I've starting giving less of a fuck at work this past week than I ever have.

It seems that I've completely checked out mentally and am no longer interested in anything that doesn't revolve around Amelia.

I don't know what that says about me, but I'm sure it can only lead to complete disaster. She'd told me more than once that her stay in the city is only temporary, but my stupid heart either refuses to listen or is purposefully ignoring her warning because it's falling anyway.

The next time I see her, I'll have to ask her where she's from. I doubt it's anywhere local, but hey, I can dream, right?

I wouldn't mind maybe a state or two away; that way I could visit whenever either of us had free time.

God, look at me, trying to plan a nonexistent future with a woman I barely know. Kylie would be having a complete field day if she saw me right now.

Heading into the bathroom, I push open the door, only to be startled that the lights are already on and the shower running. Steam billows out from above the curtain while rain pours down onto the floor of the tub as someone rinses themselves.

My heart picks up.

Did…she actually stay?

"…Amelia?"

"What?" she answers me from behind the curtain.

I literally sag against the doorframe.

She stayed.

She actually stayed.

I look up when the curtain is yanked back and her face appears. "What are you doing?"

She looks different without all of her sultry makeup, but still so damn beautiful. And is that red hair I spy? "Uh…"

"Well? Come on." She smirks at me and waves her hand. "You aren't going to keep me waiting, are you?"

God, I'm so fucking done. I'd crawl over a pit of fire for her if she asked me to.

Pushing away from the doorframe, I head over to her and take her outstretched hand. She yanks me behind the curtain and draws it back all in one motion. I stumble slightly, my shoulders bumping into the tilted wall, which draws a small laugh out of her.

She stands under the spray, stretching her arms over her head and relaxing under the hot water. Her body is even more breathtaking like this, every curve on display for me as water trails over her skin, making my mouth water.

All I want to do is lick up every last droplet and taste every soft part of her like she's the only food on Earth.

She must see the hunger in my eyes because she says, "Do you want me?"

Glancing back to her eyes, I push away from the wall to hover over her. She watches me intently, never wavering from where she's standing under the spray still. Her eyes are curious and not as guarded as they were last night—something that gives me a sense of pride.

"Yes."

"Show me."

Without breaking our eye contact, I slowly sink down to the floor of the shower and onto my knees. Her brow raises at me, but she doesn't shy away when I grab onto one of her legs, squeezing her thigh gently.

She grabs my head. "Not without permission."

"May I?"

She tilts her head but doesn't say anything more to me. I take the opportunity to move my hand up her thigh further, slightly tugging on it to part both her legs. She gasps slightly when I use my other hand to balance her and lift her leg up over my shoulder.

"Yes..." Her hands sink into my hair, tugging at the roots. "I like you on your knees like this."

Fuck, if I wasn't already hard, hearing her voice like that certainly would make me.

I press my lips to her thigh, moving up slowly while trailing kisses along the way. I suck lightly on the soft flesh, wanting to leave my mark even though I doubt she's sleeping with anyone else.

Realistically, I'm sure she could find time, but I want to delude myself into thinking I'm the only one she's seeing right now. Stupid, sure, but I want her to be mine. And only mine. But on her terms.

Her fingers tighten their hold in my hair when I brush my nose against her pussy lips, nuzzling until I can fully bury my face between her legs. Holding her hips with both of my hands, I slowly slide my tongue between her folds and lick up her until I hit her clit.

Amelia groans. "Fuck…"

God, I love those noises.

I flick my tongue around her clit a few times, feeling it pulse slightly against my lips with each draw of my tongue. She rubs her pussy against my face, bucking her hips while she tries to draw my attention down to where her juices are starting to flow.

Her taste is so addictive, like some kind of aphrodisiac, that as soon as it hits my tongue, I'm hooked. She's wet, and I love lapping up every inch of her. Her hips stutter the moment my tongue slips inside, another moan spilling out of her.

"Oh, fuck!"

I fuck her with my tongue, pulling in and out of her the same way she rode my dick last night. My nose gets buried against her clit, brushing it every single time I plunge my tongue into her. Her hips start moving again, fucking herself against me with unrestrained vigor that has my cock straining, wanting to be inside her desperately the more I taste her.

"Shit…oh shit…!" she calls out, and then her hips are shaking from her orgasm crashing into her.

I tighten my hold on her body, keeping her upright while the leg draped over my shoulder moves wildly. I turn her slightly to press her against the wall to keep her from collapsing backward. I'd probably catch her, but I don't want to take my mouth off of her until I'm forced to. I lap up all of her juices like she's the only oasis for miles.

"Jax," she moans. "Oh fuck."

I turn my attention back to her clit. Wrapping my mouth around her, I suckle on it, using the tip of my tongue to flick it as fast as I can. She cries out again, her body arching back into the wall while she holds me tight against her pussy.

I let go of one of her hips, making sure she's steady before doing so, and circle my finger around her slit. It clenches a few times at my teasing, desperately trying to push my finger inside and clamp around it before I can pull it back. With ease, I slip it inside of her, groaning when her walls immediately tighten around it.

"Yes, oh fuck. Yes, fuck me…!"

This is the first time she's letting me take this much control. Even down on my knees like this with my face shoved into her pussy, I can tell that this is something she doesn't let happen very often. I want to savor every last second I have with her throwing all of her inhibitions out the window in order for me to satisfy her.

I move my finger in a slow rhythm. The pulsating of her walls has my own hips buckling, wishing for it to be clenching around my cock instead. I sink my finger as deep as I can until my knuckles breech her.

She feels soooo fucking good.

Amelia practically ruts against me. "Yes…yes, yes…fuck, you're going to make me cum again…"

Her words are so desperate sounding that I move my finger faster in her. I want her to orgasm until she can't stand anymore, until she practically collapses over me and I can bring her back to bed and lay with her all day.

I want it all.

Amelia gasps, her body shuddering again as she cums. It milks my finger as much as it can, pulling me deep and not letting me go until it's satisfied with what it's gotten. Right on the uptick of me pulling my finger out, I decide at the last second to add another and shove them both inside of her while she's still cumming.

She cries out. "Jax!!"

I don't let up on her clit at all, continuing to suck

and flick until my lips are practically numb. I thrust in and out of her, curling my fingers with each pull to rub against the sensitive spot inside of her.

She matches each pull with her hips, slamming back into my hand like she's pretending to ride my cock. My knuckles press into her pussy each time, stopping just shy of breeching her. Over and over I drive my fingers into her, fucking her like I would with my cock until she's dripping down my fingers.

"Oh my god!!" she chokes out.

My knees are numb, but I don't care. I want her to beg for me this time.

Her body goes rigid with another orgasm; this time it crashes into her hard enough for her to choke out a gasp and slump back against the wall behind her. Her thigh twitches against my head, her walls pulsating around my fingers before she finally goes lax.

I quickly steady her with my one hand before carefully drawing my fingers out of her and grabbing onto her other hip. Her eyes are dazed when she stares down at me, her mouth slack while she drags air into her lungs.

"That..." she says after a while. "Was amazing."

CHAPTER 13

Jax

AMELIA SURPRISES me by agreeing to breakfast after we finally clean up.

I watch her over the rim of my coffee cup, the steam from it warming my face while I take her all in. She's forgone the wig today and has instead let her long and beautiful red ringlets fall over her shoulders. My fingers itch to run through the long, silky lengths, to feel them slide between my fingers and curl the ends around.

She looks different without all the severe makeup covering her features, but it's a good kind of different. She has softer features than I would've thought, her cheeks slightly rounder and her lips pouty-looking without the dark lipstick staining her skin.

But her eyes haven't changed at all. In fact, they seem much more sharp than ever. She watches me out of her peripheral, studying me carefully while she forks pieces of her egg into her mouth. I'm hyper aware of how I'm sitting and moving as I set my coffee down to eat my own breakfast. Every single miniscule movement that I make is being tracked and calculated.

I don't know why it turns me on so much to feel like I'm being stalked by a predator, but I must have some kind of thrill for danger because I can already feel my cock hardening in my pants.

"After this," Amelia finally speaks, "you're going to work?"

I look up at her, nodding. "What about you?"

Her eyes flash with amusement at my question as she grabs her glass of orange juice and brings it up to her mouth. Her gaze doesn't waver as she stares at me over the rim while she drinks. When she finally puts it back down again, she smirks.

"I have a meeting."

There's something in the way her tone shifts that has me intrigued. Obviously, if she wanted to tell me what her business was about, I'm sure she would. I haven't known Amelia for that long, but I know her well enough to realize that she's only an open book when she wants to be. She picks and chooses when to be forthcoming and is good at hiding what she wants to keep in the shadows.

A factor that only increases the mystery surrounding her, along with my attraction for her.

"Is it important?" I ask.

I know I'm fishing, but I can't help it. Everything she does interests me in the worst way. It tickles that researcher part of my brain that loves to dig and dig until I solve the issue, figure out the equation, whatever it is that Amelia's dangling in front of me right now.

She only shrugs at me, picking up a piece of her toast and taking a bite out of it. Clearly I'm not going to be getting any answers from her—which I suppose is fair enough. It's not like she owes me anything. But goddamn am I curious to know everything and anything about her.

"What about you?" She nods to me. "Is your work important?"

I pick my coffee up off the table to swirl the contents around while I think for a moment. It's not like my job *isn't* important—working directly under the district attorney isn't anything to sneeze at. I'd worked my ass off to make partner and get to where I was in my career, much to the detriment of my social and love life.

At the time, I thought it had all been worth it. I'd never been one for the simpler things in life like Kylie had always dreamed off—falling in love, getting married, starting a family, living that white picket-fenced life that was sold as the American dream.

I liked to feel on edge, an adrenaline junkie to my core, even if my outward appearance didn't exactly scream "thrill seeker." Settling down was never on my list of priorities, at least, not until this past year when my best friend and little sister had fallen in love and were currently having a baby.

For some reason, seeing them both together had given me a hard slap of reality. I'd never realized how little time I'd actually spent on myself versus putting all of my time and energy into my work and the world around me. I'd felt fulfilled in climbing to the top, but now that I was up here, I was starting to realize just how lonely it was.

A part of me regretted letting it all get to me. I was happy for my sister and my best friend, but that ugly, envious part of me that I'd never felt in my life had suddenly reared its ugly head. And now here I was, sitting across from the most interesting and beautiful woman I'd ever seen.

I had no idea how long I would get to keep seeing her, and I knew the moment we parted ways, it was going to hit me hard. I'd never been one for romantics, but damn did Amelia make it hard not to believe in that crash and burn of falling for someone so hard that it took your breath away.

As stupid as it sounded for someone like me—a level-headed lawyer who dealt with life with pure facts—it felt...*right* being here with Amelia. No matter what secrets she kept or who she really was, I wanted to know all of it. I *wanted* all of it.

"I work for the district attorney. So...yeah, I guess you could say that."

She tilts her head curiously. "What made you want to go into that?"

I shrug. "It sounds corrupt, but I like finding loopholes. That part of the law has always interested me."

A slow smile works its way onto her face. "Careful who you tell that to. You might end up being kidnapped and used for that brain of yours."

I chuckle softly. "Is that you offering?"

Her eyes flash again, this time with a darker and more devious look to them. "You wouldn't be able to handle what I've got going on, Jax. Trust me."

God, I wanted her to open up to me so fucking bad it was actually pathetic. I was a fucking dog, ready to get on my hands and knees and beg her to stay and not disappear on me again. I'd never felt this kind of need in my life to have someone around, but Amelia had a magnetic pull that I couldn't help but let myself fall into.

"That sounds like a challenge."

She leans back in her chair, her smile widening. "It isn't."

While her words say one thing, that look on her face says another. It's like she *wants* me to pry and dig for more. Like she's sliding over the invitation and silently saying, "Come look." It's fucking maddening.

Instead of falling deeper into that rabbit hole, though, I pivot the conversation. "Where are you from, Amelia? I can't quite place your accent."

"Ireland. Belfast, to be exact."

My heart stutters in my chest. "You're from out of the country?"

"Unless you have an Ireland in the U.S. that I don't know about, then yes, I am."

Damn, does that mean she's leaving the second she'd done with whatever it is she is here to do?

I try not to read too deeply into why my heart sinks at that. This arrangement between us was only ever going to be temporary, even if my stupid heart wants more. I barely know Amelia, but it feels like we've been entangled for much longer than a week at this point.

Deep down, I wish there was a way for me to get her to stay after she's done with whatever it is that she's come here to do. But it wouldn't be fair of me to ask that of her when we hardly know each other. If we were in the reverse roles, I would've thought she was crazy if she asked me to stay on foreign land for someone she just met.

At least, that's what I tell myself.

"Your family live back there as well, I presume?"

She nods.

Flicking my fingers against the side of my coffee mug, I say, "I've got a kid sister here in the city. Her and my best friend are having a baby."

There's no reason to tell her about my life, but I want to, as stupid as that sounds. I want us to get to know each other despite the temporary status hanging over us.

"Oh? That's quite scandalous."

I laugh a little. "Yeah, never expected that. But they're good for each other, so I don't really mind."

"I'm glad they're happy. Are you excited to be an uncle?"

Strangely enough, that thought hadn't quite hit me yet. Obviously, it would be inevitable that once my niece or nephew was born, I'd become one. But so far, I hadn't actually been picturing my involvement with their child out of the context of helping my sister in her recovery after the fact.

Was that bad of me? I kind of just assumed I'd see them on occasion while I swamped myself in work.

"Yes?" I finally say.

She snorts at me. "You don't seem very confident."

I shrug. "Well, I'll be there when they want me to be. I guess that's how I can put it."

Amelia nods, crossing a leg over her knee.

"What about you? Any nieces or nephews?"

"God, no. It's just my mother and me, aside from my extended family."

Lifting my mug back up again, I press the rim of the ceramic against my lips to breathe in the scent of the coffee inside. "No lover or anything back home?"

I can tell that the question is a mistake even before it leaves my mouth, but I can't do anything to stop it once it already comes tumbling out. To Amelia's credit, she doesn't scold or yell at me, but instead she leans back in her chair while a slow smirk crosses her face.

It's the look of a predator who's finally caught their prey in a trap. She waits, watching me squirm while the uncomfortable silence stretches on between us. If I had any questions about her getting off on this sort of thing—having power over men—then it's certainly been answered by now.

I hate that jealousy flares inside of my chest. It's stupid of me to assume in the first place that someone such as Amelia wouldn't ever be entertaining anyone other than just me. She was not only a bombshell and drop-dead gorgeous, she was intelligent and had an untamed quality about her that was completely unique to anyone I'd ever met.

Did I have any reason to question her relationship status? Absolutely not, but yet here I was doing just that because I secretly couldn't stand the thought of anyone else other than myself getting into bed with her, getting to know her, looking through those thin cracks in her wall that allowed me to see into who she was deep down.

"Do you really want to know the answer to that question?" she finally asks.

No, I want to say. But the envy in me has me saying something completely different. "Yes."

She lets out a laugh before pushing her plate back and standing. "Come walk me to my car."

The change is so abrupt that it has me putting my

coffee down and standing immediately. "Lead the way."

AMELIA'S CAR was actually more than just that.

I was surprised to find it idling on the curb at the front of the hotel, a man standing outside of it waiting for her and straightening up as she approached. He walked around to the rear door and opened it for her, waiting next to it while she stopped and turned back to me.

"This has been fun, Jax." She gives me a smile that's a little more devious looking than I'm expecting.

For some reason, her words have my heart sinking. "Yes, I've had fun too. Am I over-assuming by thinking this is you saying goodbye, though?"

She laughs again. "We will have to eventually."

I sigh and flit my eyes away. While it's true, I don't exactly want to think about it. As short of a time as it's been since meeting her, Amelia's changed my life completely. No longer am I the same person who day in and day out went through the rigamarole of routine just for the sake of it. I'd somehow discovered a new side of myself that I wasn't willing to let go of so easily.

It wasn't Amelia's responsibility to coax me through this change I was going through, but damn if I didn't feel attached, no matter how stupid it made me look.

"Jax." She reaches out a hand, grabbing my arm to squeeze.

About to open my mouth and ask her, "What?" I'm interrupted by another familiar voice.

"Jax?"

Craning my head around, I blink at the sudden appearance of my baby sister standing on the sidewalk a few feet from Amelia and me. She has a paper bag of groceries cradled in her arms while her eyes dart between Amelia and me. Guilt strikes me immediately as I realize I had yet to tell Kylie about this. I'd hinted at it, sure, but never had gone into my status of actually seeing someone.

"Hey." I move over to her, pulling away from Amelia. "Let me grab those for you."

She side-steps me, grinning easily. "What, you think just because I've got a bun in the oven that I suddenly can't handle carrying a bag of groceries?"

That made me want to groan and rub a hand over my face. Leave it to Kylie to completely call me out like that. "I'm just trying to help."

"Save it." She hip-checks me. "When I get big and bloated, *then* you can maybe see about carrying my groceries."

I shake my head at her before patting her on the head like we were kids. "Why are you all the way over this way?"

She narrows her eyes at me, raising a brow while she drawls out, "I could ask you the same thing."

Shit...

Behind me, I hear Amelia clear her throat. Her heels click on the sidewalk as she walks over to us, the steady sound of them matching with my pulse.

"It's nice to meet you. I'm Jade."

My head snaps around to look at her, blinking when she raises a hand to greet my sister. Kylie grins again and shifts her bag of groceries in order to grab Amelia's hand and shake it properly.

"It's nice to meet my brother's...?" Kylie trails off, looking between us again.

"Friend," Amelia finishes for her, smile widening when she drops her hand from my sister's. "I've heard quite a bit about you, actually."

"Really." Kylie looks her up and down. "Well, it's nice to finally meet you, Jade. My brother's quite a workaholic, so he doesn't get around to calling me much these days."

I wince at the subtle dig. While it's true that I am always working, I catch the underlying meaning there as well. Kylie isn't so much calling me out for working too much in general, but more jabbing at the fact that she hasn't even heard of Amelia, let alone been introduced to the idea of me seeing anyone.

"I've been busy," I say, shoving both my hands into my pockets.

My sister isn't usually one to embarrass me in

front of people, but I also know that sometimes she can be a bit of a loose cannon when it comes to that mouth of hers. She's always been one to speak her mind, even at the detriment of my ego.

Kylie raises another brow at me, winking. "Clearly *very* busy."

Ugh…here we go…

It has Amelia laughing, though, surprising us both. "While I'd love to stay and chat, I have an obligation I must attend to."

As she turns, she manages to brush against my shoulder while giving me a secretive smile that only I can see by how she's turned her body away from my sister.

"I'll see you later."

I hold back a grin, only letting myself smile slightly while I nod. "Of course. You have my number."

I hear Kylie snicker.

Ignoring her, I walk Amelia back over to her car and help her inside of it when she offers me her hand. I squeeze her fingers gently before letting her go, stepping back as the driver swings her door shut behind her. The window rolls down, and Amelia's beautiful face appears.

"See you soon," is all she says before she's whisked away.

Damn, I've got it so bad…

"Wow." I look to my left where Kylie now stands.

"What did you think?"

It isn't often that I ask for my sister's opinion on my dating life, but so far my feelings for Amelia have been incredibly jumbled. I want to know if I'm crazy for reading into her giving me signs that she's interested in me or if I'm just playing myself by thinking like that. Either way, I know this is all going to end in disaster, but the part of me that cares has completely walked out the door by now.

Kylie shrugs, shifting her bag of groceries once again. "She's certainly intimidating. How the hell did you meet someone like her? She's way out of your league."

I laugh; it's too true. Amelia really is on a completely separate level. "A bar."

She rolls her eyes at me. "Wow, and she still wants to see you? You must've impressed her."

I doubt that, but then again, why *does* Amelia want to keep spending time with me? Not to boost my ego or anything by saying I'm good in bed, but we do have ridiculous chemistry. Whatever it is that is keeping the both of us locked onto each other isn't something I'm going to complain about.

Not when it gets Amelia to keep seeing me.

"Maybe." I shrug. "We'll see, I guess."

Kylie shakes her head at me. "I'd tell you to treat her right, but she gives me the impression that she's the kind of woman that will knock you right off your feet if you piss her off enough."

I hold back a laugh because that's *exactly* what has happened already. Amelia wouldn't give two shits about knocking me down a few pegs, especially if it meant putting me back in my place.

I loved that, though. I loved the power she commanded in the face of everyone else. It was nothing like I'd ever experienced before.

I nudge my sister, breaking out of my thoughts. "Let's get you home."

CHAPTER 14

Amelia

When I meet with Kenny again, I'm surprised to see Giovani Lavin in attendance.

As satisfying as it was to see that I'd gotten the reclusive buyer out of whatever hole he usually hide himself in, I had a feeling that this meeting was going to go exactly as I was expecting it to: poorly.

Lavin wasn't known for being the most flexible when it came to negotiating over a deal that wasn't a slam dunk. He was used to people bending over backward for him and begging him for his money and attention. Personally, I would never in my life stoop to such a level.

I had pride in my products, and the deals I made were always in the benefit of myself and my family, not the other way around. As an arms supplier, it made no sense to me to be on the short end of the stick when we were the ones that provided the product necessary for the other part to make money.

What other industry worked that way? It never made any sense to me, and the fact that Lavin had been bold enough to demand such a steep profit-share markup, let alone one in general, just went to show how much of an ego the man had.

Not once had I ever been asked my terms, let alone what I was interested in getting out of this deal. Lavin wasn't interested in seeing to it that I got a fair share of the margin that he was wanting to profit from to beginning with, so why the fuck should I ever bend to his will over something like that? Especially when it comes to money.

I let the teacup in my hand rest against my knee, feeling the heat of it sink down through my pant leg. Whatever it is that Giovani Lavin thinks he can squeeze out of me is either going to make me laugh or piss me off; that much I know.

"So my associate tells me your family isn't interested in a profit share," Lavin starts, lifting his own tea to his lips to sip before he continues on. "I'm surprised. These deals are quite common in this market."

I fight the urge to roll my eyes. As if I care what the American market is like. He sought out my products for a reason, so the fact that he's trying to spin it in a way that makes the situation show that *I'm* the one chasing him is ludicrous at best.

"The Devlins don't profit share, let alone for that kind of markup."

On the other side of me, Kenny shifts slightly in

his chair. Lavin sits across from me in an oversize loveseat with high-lifting armrests that seem to cradle him into the chair. He has a leg crossed over his knee where he rests his teacup on as he regards me with a cool expression.

His pepper gray hair is pushed back from his face, the lines of a fine-toothed comb still visible. The wrinkles around his eyes deepen as he frowns at me.

"The markup is quite common here. Buyers in this country are rather expensive to work with."

I let myself lean back into the couch cushion behind me. "Then why are you wasting my time approaching someone like me from overseas for product when you seem to have your fair share of dealers here?"

I hold back a smirk as the man's frown deepens. *Gotcha.*

"You see..." He shifts the teacup slightly, spinning it on the saucer until the handle is facing the opposite way. "There have been some...rather unfortunate circumstances that have come up that have led to my trust being broken in the chain of exchange. I've decided to outsource because I believe it will be more beneficial to both parties in the long run, as well as being able to keep up a more professional relationship."

Interesting. I'm intrigued to find out just exactly what happened that made someone like Lavin no longer trust his original dealers. For someone like him to force himself to search overseas for a new dealer, it must've been bad.

I'll have to get Aidan, my temporary liaison, to dig up some dirt about that.

"I see. Unfortunately, that's not my problem."

This time, Lavin does sigh. "I'm realizing that you clearly have an idea on how you'd like this deal to go?"

Obviously…

"I'm not one to enter into a deal without a plan, no," I answer instead. "I don't do profit shares, and I don't do steep markups. You either buy my products at the cost that I sell them at, or I'm walking out that front door and not returning, and you can figure out how else you're going to be getting a supply to sell off on the black market. Either way, none of this is my problem."

Honestly, he was lucky I even took the time out of my day to meet with him in the first place. When his team had reached out to mine about the possibility of a big sale, of course I'd been eager to get over here. We'd needed a good buyer that was interested in a long-term contract overseas.

My mother had been encouraging me to branch out for a while now, and this had been the perfect opportunity to do so. However, if I knew it was going to be this much of a headache, I wouldn't've bothered.

"What about negotiating down the markup?"

I shook my head. “Either you take what I’m giving you or I walk. It’s that simple.”

These kinds of shakedowns were common, especially when dealing with old-school men like Lavin. He wasn’t used to a strong and powerful woman commanding a room, let alone strong-arming a deal and not backing down when there was a conflict in the negotiation process.

Too bad for him, I wasn’t desperate to sell my product, let alone to someone like him.

There’s an uncomfortable silence that settles over all three of us. Both Kenny and Lavin share glances, a silent argument brewing between them that I really don’t have time for. I’m wasting precious days that I could be spending with my mother, and instead I’m here dealing with this shit.

Leaning over, I set my untouched tea down and stand. “Since we can’t reach an agreement, I’ll be going.”

“Wait.” Lavin jerks forward, some of his tea spilling onto his pressed pants. He doesn’t seem to notice it, though. “What about a thirty percent profit share? And full market value for the product.”

“I’m not interested.”

“Twenty-five?”

God, this guy is actually *that* desperate. I almost feel sorry for him.

“Since you seem to enjoy wasting my time,” I drawl, “I now want an extra five percent on the markup as a tax for beating around the bush so much, as well as zero percent profit share."

Out of the corner of my eye, Kenny's mouth drops open.

I smirk. "Take it or leave it."

We'll see how desperate this man really is.

There's a loud silence that hangs over us all again, one that has Kenny shifting in his seat uncomfortably. Lavin fixes me with a glare, the muscles in his jaw moving as he grits his teeth together in agitation. Whatever, he can be mad all he wants. If he's that set on buying from me, he's going to have to pay for it.

"Fine," he finally says.

"B-But sir," Kenny swings up to his feet, "we should talk about this."

Lavin holds up a hand, his eyes closing while he sighs heavily. "Enough."

I'm dying of curiosity—clearly whatever deal was going down on Lavin's end was big enough and important enough for him to be this set on getting what he needed. Which meant he must be on some kind of tight deadline or else it wouldn't make sense for him to be so hellbent on not finding another supplier and sticking with me.

As egotistical as it is to think that my family's artillery is superior, there are bigger things at play here.

"Great." I smile. "I'll have the invoice sent over immediately. Once it's paid, I'll have a crew come and drop everything off at whatever location you specify."

Lavin pulls himself to his feet, nodding while extending his hand out to me. "Thank you…for your business."

I all but grin. That satisfaction feels even better than making a sale. "It's nice doing business with you."

Lavin frowns, his hand tightening around mine as I grasp his. He holds back whatever it is he wants to say and instead gives my hand a firm shake before letting me go.

"I look forward to hearing from you."

I'M in such a good mood as I get back to my hotel room that I pull out my phone and text Jax to meet me at the bar. The weight that's been on my shoulders for the past week and a half has finally been lifted, and now I can finally breathe again.

Of course, I still have a few more days here until I can get the money from Lavin's accounts wired over to mine and the weapons shipped to whatever location he wants them at. Until then, I'm free to do as I please, which includes going on and playing around with Jax for a while.

It's sort of like my own personal celebration. Finally, I'll be able to get back to my home country and my family after being away from them for so long.

A part of me is a little sad to be leaving Jax behind, though. While I'm not exactly attached to him, I've grown fond of him, and he's been an incredible distraction. Still, I can enjoy my time with him while I have it.

I don't bother looking at my phone when I hear my text notification come in. I already know it's Jax confirming our plans without needing to look at my phone at all. I know for a fact he's as eager to see me as I am him, which is only going to make tonight even better.

I'm ready to get him under me again and finally take things to the next level.

Anticipation sends a shiver up my spine as I head into the bathroom to get ready. Tonight, I'll wear my long dark wig that will be coupled with smokey eye makeup. I want Jax to see me and fall to his knees in front of me, begging to let me fuck him. He's so fun when he's like that.

Though, I do have to say, him taking over in the shower this morning was hot as hell. Maybe we'll have to do that again too.

It takes me about an hour to get ready. By then, the sun has already started to set outside of my windows, casting a warm glow over my hotel room. Slipping on a pair of heels and grabbing my purse and phone, I head out the door and call for a car to come around and pick me up.

I check my phone on the way down inside of the elevator, spotting Jax's *"can't wait"* flashing across my screen as I text back my driver. Despite myself, I smile at my phone.

I'd been surprised when his sister had shown up earlier, startling us both out of our conversation. She seemed nice enough, even though she'd given me the third degree with her eyes. I didn't blame her, though. I doubted Jax mentioned me at all to her, let alone how often we'd been seeing each other the past week.

This was all still so relatively new that I wouldn't be surprised if he kept the information from her. It wasn't like we were dating, anyway, so there was no point in telling her the truth. Plus, it wouldn't surprise me if she was the type to balk at her brother getting down and dirty with a stranger like me—especially one that could kill him with something as simple as a pillow.

Nevertheless, I could tell that Jax cared about her. That much was evident in the way he doted on her, even in the small few-minute window I'd spent together with them.

It reminded me of my own brother and his protectiveness over me when he'd still been alive.

Once I get down to the lobby, I head out the front doors and into the awaiting car. As the door shuts behind me, I quickly text Jax that I'm on my way and lean back into the seat behind me. Thinking about the few days we have left together, I want to make the most of our time now that I don't have to worry about that deal.

Looking at my window, I see my reflection staring back at me and smile just a little.

I'm ready for tonight.

CHAPTER 15

Amelia

I'M ABOUT HALFWAY through a martini when Jax finally arrives.

He's in his typical suit—his office wear tailored to him in a way that cuts him just right. Everyone in the bar turns to stare at him, women wanting a piece of him and men sizing him up as they swirl their beers in their half-empty glasses.

There's power in capturing a man like that's attention. A kind of notoriety that isn't easily replicated, nor is it easily ignored.

Jax spots me and smiles to himself as he heads over. Eyes trail after him and over to me, the dots suddenly connecting. As a couple, we make sense. We both stand out in these kinds of settings, even when I want to remain more low key. I can't help it if my sex appeal is usually off the charts even with my disguises, and Jax's innate appeal is obvious.

When he grabs a chair from another table next to

mine, he drags it over and settles down onto it. Leaning back, he hooks his ankle over his knee and gives me a nice, long once-over.

"I like this one."

My lashes flutter, my hand reaching out to grab my glass and swirl the rest of the liquor inside of it. "I'm sorry, do I know you?"

He chuckles. "No, but I'd like to get to know you."

Cheesy…I kind of like it.

Right as I'm about to open my mouth to retort back, I feel my phone vibrate inside of my purse that's pressed up against my leg. I'm not expecting any calls, which can only mean one thing: there's something wrong.

Picking up my bag, I place it in my lap before flicking the clasp open and rooting around the inside. My phone is still going off by the time I find it, the screen flashing with my mother's contact for a split second before it disappears and the entire screen goes black.

Weird…she never calls me this late.

Unlocking my phone and hitting the option to call her back, I put the speaker up to my ear and listen to the dial tone.

What I'm not expecting is the person to pick up the other line to not be my mother, but my uncle instead.

"Amelia?"

His voice has me frowning. "Why do you have her phone?"

I'm careful not to say anything in front of Jax, who is giving me a curious look.

"There's… You need to come home."

A sudden dark feeling comes over me. "Why? What happened?"

"It's better if I explain it to you in person."

Alarms go off in my head immediately. "Why do you have her phone?"

My uncle sighs at me. "Amelia…"

"Answer me. Why do you have her phone?"

No...no, no, no, my mind chants at me. She's fine, she has to be. Maybe she fell and hurt herself and was headed to the hospital or there was some kind of attack on the estate and now they were having to shut everything down to keep everyone safe and needed me home to take care of things.

It had to be. I wouldn't accept anything else.

"Amelia. Please."

"Tell me," I snapped. My throat was already beginning to get tight.

He let out another sigh. "She's gone."

The words completely shatter my heart. All of the air in the bar has been sucked out, leaving me feeling breathless as I try to fight for my body to breathe. I had to have heard wrong. She isn't gone. She's still here. I would've felt if she…if she…

"She passed about two hours ago. I wanted to call you and tell you so we can start making arrangements."

Oh god.

Oh my god.

I grip the side of the table hard enough to hurt my hands, forcing myself to remain restrained before I completely lose it in the middle of this fucking bar and in front of Jax, who is staring me down.

I know I'm shaking, but I keep my voice even as I speak. "I'll be on a plane tonight."

"Good. I'll send a car to come get you. And Amelia?"

"What?"

He pauses. "I'm sorry."

I end the call before I say things I know I'll regret later. Taking out my anger, my complete devastation on my mother's only brother won't do anyone any good. I need to keep my head on straight in order to make it back to Ireland or I am going to have the biggest meltdown of my life and be confined to a bed for the rest of the week, unable to move.

I need to be over there—to see for myself—that she is really gone.

"…Amelia? You all right?"

Finally pulling in a breath, I squeeze my eyes shut and will my tears back into the ducts.

How am I going to live without her? How am I supposed to navigate the rest of my life without my mother?

The thoughts rattle me to my core.

Oh god, I can't do this.

A hand grasps one of mine, prying it from the side of the table. "What happened? What can I do?"

I snatch it back from his like it burns me. *"Don't."*

He flinches in surprise, leaning back to give me room to breathe. He doesn't say anything while he watches me pant like a lunatic, my body so desperate for oxygen it looks like I've just run a marathon.

Pushing up from my seat, my knees buckle under me, causing me to pitch forward and catch myself on the side of the table. Jax reaches out immediately, taking me by the shoulder and helping me stand up straight. I'm shaking so badly that my teeth are chattering.

Pull it together.

She can't be gone. She can't be.

"Let me get you back to your hotel room." His voice is full of concern, and even without looking at him, I know there's a worried frown on his face. He's so predictable. "My car's outside—"

"Airport," I mumble.

"What?" He leans in closer to hear me.

"Air. Port."

There's a beat of hesitation that almost causes me to turn and yell at him, but he's moving before I get a chance to form the words. Jax grabs my purse and shoves my phone into it before snapping it closed. He takes me by the arm and all but drags me out of the bar and down the sidewalk.

I'm barely conscious honestly, my vision pin pricking and my head dizzy from the information overload. I have so many questions but not a single desire for the answers.

Did she suffer? How did it happen? Who found her? What did she look like?

All of them swirl around in my head like a hamster wheel.

I blink, and suddenly I'm in the passenger seat of Jax's car. He leans across me and buckles me, strangely aware that I've checked out. When he shuts my door and heads around the front hood to climb into his own seat, I suddenly remember that I need to book a ticket to actually go anywhere.

"Bag," I tell him the second he's sliding into the driver's side.

He doesn't ask me anything stupid and grabs it from the back seat, placing it in my lap before slamming his door shut and buckling in himself. I rip my bag open, dumping the contents of it onto my lap, some of it spilling onto the floor, and grab my phone before it slips off my lap.

"Want me to…?" he offers.

"No," I snap at him, my fingers shaking as I pull up a search engine and look for the soonest available flight.

Jax nods to me and turns the car on before shifting it into gear and heading off. I barely register the drive at all, too consumed with my phone and booking myself a flight that by the time I lift my head, we're already idling at the drop-off.

Out of the corner of my eye, I can see Jax staring at me again.

"What happened, Amelia?" His voice is soft. I hate it.

Tears burn in my eyes again. "...My mother is dead."

I try to say it with the least amount of emotion as I possibly can, but it comes out sounding strained and barely contained. I can't do this; I can't go back to Ireland just to bury her in a box on my family's plot of land. I can't say goodbye to her when I never got the chance to see her before I left.

I'm a horrible daughter. I should've cut the deal and run when I had the chance. Instead, I let my stupid pride get in the way.

"I'm so sorry," he tells me—words I absolutely fucking hate.

It's like my brother and father's funeral all over again. All the "my condolences" and "I'm sorrys" driving me to insanity while the impersonal handshakes left me feeling too exposed.

And now I'm going to have to do it all over again.

"I can walk you in."

I shake my head, letting out a small sigh. "I don't want you to."

"Amelia—"

"Jax. Please. Please don't. Not right now."

He squeezes the steering wheel. "I can head over to your hotel room and get you your things and send them to you. Just give me your key card and whatever address you want them sent to."

I shake my head. "I have people for that."

"People?" he repeats to himself.

Unhooking the seatbelt from around me, I bend and gather all of my things that spilled out of my purse and shove it back inside before clasping it closed. I don't want to look at his face, can't stand seeing the sympathy on it, so I don't. I turn to the door and pops it open, slowly stepping out into the cool night air.

Jax is already getting out of his side, his hazards flashing and lighting up the curb by his rear bumper. He comes around to stand by me, his hand hovering near me in order to catch me in case I fall.

"Tell me what I can do."

"Go home," I tell him. "Just...forget any of this happened. Please." I hate how choked up I sound. "Forget about me and pretend none of this ever happened."

I walk away from him, ignoring him calling out to me one last time before heading into the double-wide sliding doors. I hold my head up high and head over to the counter to get back to my home country.

I only have a limited amount of time before shit hits the fan and I'm sunk before I can even get a chance to get a life raft to safety. There's no time to waste—even as I feel my heart trying to crack through my ribs and bleed all over the ground.

CHAPTER 16

Jax

I DON'T HEAR from Amelia for days afterward.

She consumes my thoughts, keeping me up at night and filling my dreams every time I close my eyes. That devastated expression on her face was all I could remember of her—no longer was she the sexy bombshell I knew her as, but instead, she was broken and trying to hold it together.

It killed me not to know what happened to her, especially with her phone now disconnected after the fifth time of me trying to call her. I had a feeling that the number she'd been using had been an American-only line, and now that it was no longer in service, I had no other way to reach her to make sure she was all right.

Even though I barely knew her, she was still special to me. She and I had met for a reason, and I couldn't help but feel guilty about leaving her back at that airport after she'd heard what sounded like horrible news.

I'd watched her entire world crumble right before my eyes, and what did I do? I left her.

Even now, I want to kick myself.

Work as well as other mundane things pass me by without a single second thought for them. Kylie called a few times to check on me—somehow sensing through our weird sibling connection that something was off about me—but even as she tried her best, she couldn't get it out of me.

How was I supposed to tell her that a girl I barely knew was halfway across the globe in distress and I wanted to do something stupid like drive to the airport and get the first ticket to Ireland that I possibly could?

Did I have any idea where the fuck Amelia could be? No, not at all. But that didn't stop the intrusive thoughts either.

I soon found myself looking up flight tickets for Belfast in the middle of my work day anyway. Which, to my surprise, was a huge city.

Of course it was...

No sooner did I close out of the window for the third time that morning did one of my coworkers, Lionel, knock on my office door with a stack of papers in his hands. "Got these sent over for you to look at."

I sigh, rubbing my face with my hands. I'm really not in the mood today...

"Uh-oh, I know that look," he says, walking into my office. I hear the sound of a hundred papers slapping down on my desk before I peek at him through my fingers. "A girl broke your heart, huh?"

Under my hands, I make a face. "What?"

He nods to me. "Trust me, I've seen enough heartbroken young men to be an expert at this by now."

I sigh. "I'm not heartbroken."

Even to me, though, it sounds unconvincing. Lionel raises a brow at me as I lean back from my desk and settle against the back of my chair. I'm already so fucking tired, and it's barely even ten thirty. It also hasn't helped that the last time I got sleep was the night before Amelia left.

Since then, I'm lucky if I've gotten four hours.

"What was her name?"

You know what? If I deny it anymore, he's just going to keep bothering me.

With another sigh, I say, "Amelia."

"Pretty. This girl got a last name too?"

"Why, you going to try and stalk her online?"

Lionel grins at me. "Maybe. I could probably find out if she ditched you for a boyfriend or something."

Honestly, the thought had crossed my mind, as brief as it was. I doubted that it was true, though, given the way Amelia had reacted to whatever it was the person on the other side of the phone had told her. She didn't strike me as the type to get upset over something mundane like a boyfriend or whatever else of that nature.

All I knew was that she'd held herself together long enough to leave and never look back. While I admired the strength, I can't help but feel like I should've done more for her. The least I could've done was walk her into the damn airport.

"She's from Ireland," I finally say. "Last name's Devlin."

"Oh, that's a clan name. You got yourself a princess, eh?" As Lionel smiles, the gap between his two front teeth show.

A princess?

"Don't see what a princess would be doing over here in the States," I drawl.

He laughs at me. "It's just a figure of speech. What I mean to say is old names like that—clan names—they're old school. Go by their own rules type thing. When I went over to visit my nan in Ireland late last year, she was telling me all about it. Guess she knows a gal that was seeing some boy from the O'Conner clan a while back. Didn't end well, from what I heard."

That has me blinking in surprise. "Didn't end well as in...?"

"They got chopped up and thrown in the river. Terrible stuff."

What?

I shake my head to myself. While I was suspicious of Amelia's identity and her real motive for coming over to the States, I doubted she was into that kind of lifestyle.

Though…even as the thought occurred to me… was that even true? Amelia was such a mystery that maybe she was a part of some deadly clan that frequented rivers with body bags in tow. I'd never seen a gun on her person, but the more I thought about her, the more I could definitely see her having the confidence in carrying one—even going so far as to shoot it at someone.

But why in the world would she have been over here in the States? What would've been her motivation? There weren't old clans like Irish or even Mexican here. We had gangs, but that was about it. There was no old culture that went back centuries, nothing that tied people together like a bloodline and the honor of being a part of something.

I had never heard of the last name Devlin in any capacity, though that didn't mean much anyway. I was just some lawyer that worked for the state. I'd dealt with gang violence for a lot of my career, but it was nothing an organized as what Lionel was suggesting.

"What else have you heard about the Devlins?" I ask him.

He shrugs. "Nothing much. Doubt you'll find anything online. They're those types that like to move in the shadows. Think of those old samurai clans out in the East back in the day. That's what you'd be dealing with. But instead of swords, they'd be carrying guns."

Interesting.

Had something happened to Amelia's family that had caused her to have to ditch whatever she was doing here and run back home? It certainly seemed like that kind of emergency. And from what Lionel was suggesting, and my knowledge of gangs in general, perhaps there had been some kind of turfy dispute going on that ending in a tragedy.

That would certainly explain Amelia's devastation at the news.

So then who really was Amelia Devlin? *Was* she a clan princess or something to the same effect?

My head was really spinning.

"You have any way to get in contact with your girl?" Lionel asks.

I shake my head. "Her phone got disconnected. It was a U.S. number, though, so I'm not surprised."

He nods. "Any idea where she went?"

"Back home, but I have no idea where that is."

He grins. "You could always ask."

That has me raising my brow again. "What do you mean? I doubt the desk agent is going to have any clue as to what I'm talking about when I mention Amelia's name."

He laughs at me. "That's not what I meant. I mean, go over to Ireland and ask around until you find the Devlin clan. Even if you find an ancestor living in the city, I don't doubt they wouldn't know their ancestry line. You can trace through an entire family once you're over there. They keep records of that, unlike us."

That...was actually a fair point.

Any European country was excellent at their record keeping. I bet I could even find someone in Belfast that was able to do a county search for any Devlins in the area. While it might not lead me directly to Amelia, it would get me somewhere.

I had to try. I can't get it out of my head that she needs me somehow—as stupid and hero-complex as that sounds.

"Thank you, Lionel."

He reaches over my desk and slaps me hard on the shoulder. "Keep me updated. Now I want to know what happens."

"Promise I'll try."

AFTER TALKING to HR about getting an extended leave, I find myself back at my apartment packing my bag.

How long I'll be gone, I have no idea, but I had plenty of time saved up to take at least a month off. I hope I find her before that happens, but at least there's a cushion.

In the back of my mind, the nagging voice in my head tells me that there isn't even a guarantee that she'll be found anyway, something that I quickly shove back and lock inside of a box. I didn't want to think like that, especially with me going to such great lengths to find her in the first place.

Was this plan entirely stupid? Of course it was. There's no denying that at all.

However, I can't help but feel my heart pick up the moment I zip my bag up and my phone chimes with the arrival of my Uber. I'll have to tell Kylie about where I'm going once I'm on the plane or else she's liable to show up at my apartment and talk me out of this whole thing.

She can be surprisingly convincing when she wants to be, and couple that with being pregnant is a whole recipe for disaster on my end.

So I don't invite the confrontation.

It's hours later that I find myself at the airport, waiting in a small chair while facing the gate to my one-way trip to Ireland, with my laptop on my lap as my fingers scroll along my trackpad while I try to desperately look up any information I can about the Devlin family.

True to what Lionel told me, there really isn't much aside from a small pub that's been named after them that is known for their craft beer. It has me sighing and flipping my laptop closed, feeling like a complete and utter mess while the gate attendant starts calling for boarding.

Slipping my laptop back in my bag, I grab my phone from my pocket and scroll through my contacts until I hit my sister's. After getting my boarding pass scanned, I head down the gateway to get onto the plane, nodding to both flight attendants who smile at me as I pass by them.

Since this was a long flight, I'd opted for first class, knowing that if I got stuck in coach while being this tense, I'd probably lose my mind on someone. After getting my bag up above me, I take a seat in my spacious chair and hit send on my phone's screen before putting it up to my ear.

It rings twice before my sister answers. "Awww, are you calling to take me out to lunch?"

Of course food is the first thing she thinks about. "No, actually."

"Ugh, lame. You'll treat me to dinner, though?"

"Actually, I won't be in the country by that point."

There's a beat of silence on the other end before my sister explodes with, "What?!"

"Some business overseas came up, so I'm on a flight over to Europe."

"Uh, what the fuck, Jax? When did this happen? What business?"

Honestly, I hadn't thought ahead of time to field these questions, but the lies come naturally. Being a lawyer has its perks, after all.

"Some client overseas needs me to meet them there. Apparently there's been a dispute with the countersuit he's filing, and I need to meet with him before the trial starts, but he's stuck over in Europe because of a passport mix up."

"Oh..." I can tell she's trying to see through the

lie, but I'm too good at weaving my words for her to really suspect anything specific. "Well…when are you coming back?"

"I'm not sure. It depends on how long it takes for me to go through all of the case files."

"Ugh, you're not going to be gone for more than a few weeks right?"

Her worried tone has me suddenly second guessing my plan. Is it wise of me to leave my pregnant sister behind? Sure, she's got Jonathan, but what if something happens? What if they need me?

Guilt sinks in my stomach, making me frown. "I'm not sure. But hey, if anything comes up, just call me all right? I'll be on a plane that day."

"…You sure?"

"Yes, absolutely. Anything at all, just call me."

Kylie laughs. "Okay, okay. Fine. Have fun being stuck in an office all day. And make sure you come back with a souvenir for the baby."

That has me smiling. "Of course."

"And call me when you land so I know your plane didn't crash into the ocean!"

I roll my eyes. Leave it to Kylie to think of the worst-case scenario. "You got it."

"Bye, love you!"

"Bye, I love you too."

Ending the call, I stare at the screen where my baby sister's caller ID photo is pictured on the screen. She's smiling at the camera with a big stuffed plush in her arms—something I won her back last year at the county fair we'd traveled out of the city to go to.

We'd even dragged Jonathan along and laughed when we'd gotten back to the car to see him sunburned beyond belief. It had been a fun day and is still one of my favorite memories.

I tap the button on the side of my phone, locking it before pocketing it again. People mill about the aisle next to me, heading toward the back of the plane, while outside of the window next to me, the ground crew goes through their final checks.

I really hope I'm making the right decision in going to Ireland. And I really hope I can find Amelia there among the hundreds of thousands of people living in that city.

Because if I don't, I know I'm going to spend the rest of my life regretting it.

CHAPTER 17

Jax

THE TRIP over to Europe is thankfully uneventful.

Aside from one of the flight attendants giving me the wrong drink—alcohol instead of the soda like I'd wanted, but had been a welcomed surprise anyway—it went smoothly.

Getting into the airport was a chore, but after getting through baggage claim, I was finally free to do what I wanted. Aimlessly, I stand in the middle of one of the front lobbies, looking out the massive floor-to-ceiling windows that face the city street.

People come and go around me, their destinations already preplanned and in motion while I stand here looking like a complete fool. I can see cabs coming up to grab travelers, and for a second, I contemplate going outside and getting into one.

But where the hell would I even go? Now that I'm finally here, I'm starting to realize what a massive oversight this has all been. I let Lionel get into my head about getting over here and finding Amelia, thinking that it'd be somehow easy. Standing in front of this window and seeing all of the city buildings peeking up over the parking garage a ways away from the front entrance, I know I'm in over my head.

Sighing, I turn and head over to one of the lounge chairs I spot over by the recharge station. My body all but collapses into it, exhaustion from traveling already taking over and weighing me down.

This had been a colossally stupid plan. Now I'm going to have to think up a way to avoid my sister for the next week or two so that she doesn't question me on when I went to Ireland and back in a day.

Leaning forward, I put my head in my hands to massage my throbbing temples. I can't admit to the truth; it's way too embarrassing at this point.

"Excuse me, sir." I feel a tap on my knee, forcing me to look up. "Are you in need of assistance?"

A man, in his older forties, smiles down at me. His trimmed white beard stands out from his darker tanned skin, his accent a heavy Irish one that's a little hard to understand. Blinking a few times to get my thoughts in order, I sit back and press my back to the chair behind me, rubbing my thighs with my hands.

"I'm just traveling."

"Yes, I see that." He taps at the small badge pinned to his chest with a name on it, Neil. "I'm a travel advocate. Are you here for business or pleasure? Either way, I can help you get to your destination."

Now that I think about it, maybe I am due for a vacation. Staying here in Ireland for a week wouldn't hurt to get my mind off things. And who knows? Maybe by a fucking stroke of luck, I'll end up running into Amelia on the streets. It's highly unlikely, but I should enjoy my time here regardless.

"I'm not sure where I'm staying yet," I answer instead. "Would you be able to help me find accommodations?"

His eyes brighten. "Certainly. Have you got any idea on where you want to stay?"

"Here in the city is fine."

"Excellent. Why don't you follow me over to my desk and we'll sit down and get you booked with something?"

I nod to him and sweep my bag up off the floor, following him across the lounge area and over to the other side where the ticket counters are all lined up together. At the far end of it is a small booth with a "TRAVEL INFORMATION" sign over it and two chairs stationed in front of the desk.

Neil pats one of the chairs before unlatching a portion of the desk in order to scoot behind it. "Do you have any plans for activities in the city at all? I can search through our accommodations based on what you'll be doing."

I take a seat at the same time he does, slinging my bag into the empty seat next to me. "Not really. I came here on a whim."

"Oh, an adventurous traveler! We don't see many

of your type nowadays. Everyone's always so busy coming and going, they never stop to enjoy the beauty of the city."

My eyes gaze back over the hustle and bustle of the airport's lobby. I can see that; at least I'll be an easy client for this guy to work with seeing as I've got no specifications for anything. I'd be good with a bed and a hot shower by the end of this.

"All right, let's see. You have an ID on you? Just so I can book through your information and not have to ask you over and over again."

I nod and stand to shove my hand down into my pocket. At least this guy is helpful. Since I had no plans on coming here and had been too worked up on the plane ride to really think about anything other than Amelia, I'd at least be able to get what sounds like an entire itinerary handed to me before walking out of here.

Who knows? Maybe I'll be feeling frisky and go sightsee like a real tourist.

I slap my ID onto the counter in front of him, my brows furrowing when the dull sound of metal clangs against the lacquered wood. Right as Neil grabs my ID do I realize that the business card Amelia had given me has somehow stuck to the other side of it.

"Oh," I say, reaching over to grab it from Neil's hand. "Let me—"

The man's eyes widen when he flips over my ID, his eyes landing on the card. When his mouth drops open and a small gasp escapes him, then I start questioning things. Never had I seen someone react that way to seeing a—what I consider—muted business card. Sure, the thing is metal and has Amelia's name and number on it, but there's nothing else on it that should warrant that expression.

Right?

"I can take that back." I offer out my hand to him.

"You…" Neil visibly swallows, his voice dropping. "You're with the Devlins."

My entire body freezes. "…You know them?"

Neil stares at me, his eyes practically bulging out of his head. He says nothing else, other than to stare me down with what I can only figure is a terrified look. Lionel's words come back into my mind, reminding me of Ireland's rich history and that last names here have power.

"Can you get me to them?" I ask instead. Hope flutters in my chest.

He swallows again, nodding slightly. "Y-yes, sir. I… Of course I can. I'll call for a car right now."

He quickly hands my ID and business card back to me, his hands shaking visibly as he grabs the corded phone off his desk and dials an in-house line. I sit back down into my chair, pocketing my things again and listen to him as he speaks quietly into the phone. When he hangs up, his face has grown pale enough where I'm a little concerned.

"How do you know them?" I ask.

He shakes his head. "Listen, is this your first time here? For them?"

The question throws me off more than it should. But I decide to be honest with him and nod. There isn't much information he can get out of me, anyway, even if this was some kind of trap—which I doubt it is. He looks way too scared to call for the police to come take me away, and again, even if they did, I would have nothing to say.

"That card." He leans over his desk, his voice barely above a whisper. "You don't show that to anyone else, you hear me? You'll wind up getting yourself into a whole mess of trouble if you go flashing something like that around here in this city. Whatever dealings you've got with the Devlins, you keep 'em to yourself. You hear me?"

I nod slowly. There's so much I want to ask, but Neil's already leaning back away from me and clamming up again. He blows out a breath and retrieves a tissue from the small box on his desk to dab at his forehead that's already begun to grow slick with sweat.

Honestly, I feel bad about freaking him out so much, but it's been worth it. I'm getting to Amelia, it seems, one way or another.

And that's all I can really hope for.

It isn't long before a man in a tailored suit and a tweed cap comes in through one of the double doors and heads over to us. He nods to Neil before stopping next to the chair occupying my bag, looking down at me curiously.

"Are you Jackson?"

I nod and stand, holding out my hand for him to shake. He merely stares down at it before bypassing my hand and grabbing onto the handle of my bag instead.

"Follow me. I've got a car outside waiting for ye."

For some reason, this man gives me a strange vibe. Like I'm somehow walking into the lion's den if I choose to follow him. He continues to stare me down, almost as if daring me to grab my bag away from him and tell him, "Never mind."

Unfortunately, I've never been raised a quitter. And if this gets me one step closer to Amelia, then I'm taking it.

Lion's den be damned.

CHAPTER 18

Amelia

As soon as my mother was gone and buried six feet in the ground, I knew I had limited time before our family was struck by an opportunistic hand.

Word of the death of my mother, if it hasn't already, will begin to circulate, and the longer I sit with idle fingers, the worse the oncoming hostile takeover will be. The Devlins have too many valuable assets for other families to not come after, especially now that the head is gone.

My mother was never the only one keeping this family together, but her place at the head has been invaluable nonetheless. After my father and brother's passing and only leaving me and her as the next in line, she'd put up a valiant fight.

Now all in vain, is what my mind supplies me with as I pour over the documents in her office, ledgers upon ledgers sprawled out before me with handwriting I can barely read scribbled all over them.

It's an unhelpful thought, but one I've been having a lot recently over the past few days. I hate that I'm going to regret not seeing her during her final days for the rest of my life and that the last thing she'd told me in our last conversation was that she'd wanted me to take care of myself.

There were so many "what ifs" and "if only I coulds" that were floating around in my head every single morning that by now I've been driven half-insane by. No amount of my staring at my own reflection in the mirror has helped, though, so diving into work and burying myself in it has been a wonderful distraction.

A knock at the office door has me sighing and lifting my head up from all of the paperwork. "What?"

"Ma'am, there's someone here to see you," a muffled voice says on the other side.

I rub my face and groan into my hands. As if I don't have enough to deal with, now that I'm acting at the head of the family until it can become a permanent position, I'm already getting calls for meetings.

Too bad no one has any common decency to let a daughter grieve before she's thrown into the chaos of the underground world.

"Send them up," I call back at the door.

"Of course. I'll send him up."

Leaning back in my chair again, I stare up at the ceiling. Whatever this is, it better be good. I don't have time to field any stupidity while I'm trying to wade through the legalities left over after my mother. So far, I've found nothing to contest my takeover of the family business, but that doesn't mean someone out there wading in the waters isn't ready to exploit some loophole in order to steal it right from under my nose.

I need to find it and squash it before someone else does.

My uncle had come around early this morning sniffing for information I hadn't been willing to give him just yet. It wasn't that I didn't trust him, but I knew that he wasn't the best at keeping his trap shut when it came to important matters like this.

Not only was this situation a delicate subject, but if *anything* got slipped out to our enemies by accident, I would pay for it.

Most likely with my life.

There is another knock on the door. "Ma'am. Your guest is here."

Guest? I puzzle. What a weird way to phrase someone coming in for a meeting. A sliver of annoyance threads through me. Is this a subtle way to dig at me for being a woman? Only having "guests" over and not clients or other big wigs that I associated with?

My mother had always struggled with the grapple of fighting for her position after my father died. She'd made it look easy, but as I grew older, I knew the constantly talk behind her back got to her.

She was the strongest woman I knew, and still, I knew that sometimes it threatened to crumble her.

Thankfully, she's taught me well. I have a much thicker skin for bullshit.

"Come in," I call and stand up from my desk, coming around to receive this "guest."

Whoever the fuck it is, they better not piss me off. My tolerance for bullshit is close to zero at this point.

When the door swings open, I stop right as I reach the twin couches facing each other and lean against the single chair at the head of them that used to be my father's preferred spot. Leaning my arm against the back of it, I spot one of my butlers in the doorway.

He bows to me before stepping back and waving his hand at my supposed guest, gesturing for them to come in.

Who walks through the office door is someone I never expected to see again.

"Jax?"

He stops short at seeing me, blinking his eyes a few times as if *he's* the one that can't believe his eyes. Like he's somehow stumbled his way onto the grounds of the Devlin estate by accident and simply walked through the doors no problem.

What the fuck!?

Finally, he relaxes. "Amelia."

I'm too stunned to even speak.

So, instead, I march over to him and yank him

into the office before slamming the door closed behind him. It rattles slightly on its hinges from the force.

"What the fuck are you doing here? Actually, no." I wave my hands in the air. "How the *fuck* did you find this place?"

"A car drove me here," is his short and simple answer. As if that tells me *anything*.

"How?" I grit through my teeth.

How the hell did he find me? I was so careful back in the States to not leave a trace of who I was. Or a trail for that matter...

What he does next shocks me more than anything that could come spouting out of his mouth. He shoves a hand into his pocket and grabs something before holding it out to me to show me. In his hand is the card—*my card*—that I gave him all those nights ago.

"At the airport, someone recognized it and brought me here," he says.

I stare at it longer than I should.

I'm going to have to send someone to that damn airport to scour it and see who the fuck is giving out information on where my family's estate is and willingly letting tourists come waltzing up to the front doors.

"Who drove you here?" I crowd into his space, not caring that I'm practically spitting the questions out at him. He's great target practice for my uninhibited rage.

"Some guy in a hat." He shrugs. "He dropped me off at the front gates. I showed your card to the guys down there, and they let me in and drove me up. This place is insane, you know that, right? You have a damn fountain and a courtyard."

I grit my teeth again. "Yes, I'm aware of what I have. I *live* here."

"I know. I'm just saying—"

I hold up my hand. "Enough, Jax. *Why* are you here?"

He frowns, dropping his hand back down at his side. "I wanted to make sure you were okay. I regretted how we left things. You weren't answering your phone. I know it's crazy I came here, but I wanted to make sure you were all right."

I hate that I'm touched by that. In reality, he's been the only one to actually go through the efforts of checking up on me. Everyone else has been busy trying to keep the business from destabilizing while I try and work out how to take over all of my family's accounts before someone else does.

It's been a slow process that's taken me more time that I care to admit to.

"Amelia?"

I look up, suddenly realizing that I've stared into space. "What?"

Without warning, he folds his arms around me and pulls me against his chest. The hug is completely unexpected but warm and inviting. He holds me in a tight and firm grip, rubbing my back gently while his cheek rests on top of my face.

"I'm sorry," he says softly. "For what happened. You don't need to tell me anything, and you can kick me out afterward. But I just wanted to make sure you got home safely and were okay."

For the first time in my entire life, a man's words choke me up. Tears burn at the corners of my eyes, most likely left over from watching my mother's casket be lowered into the ground and remaining as stone faced as possible while the rest of my entire family watched me with unabashed pity.

I could be a mess in private, but that was about it. Never once had I wanted to show weakness in front of any of them—not wanting to give anyone a reason to contest my succession any more than arbitrary and outdated rules were already actively working against me.

If I needed to remain cold and efficient in public in order to keep my temporarily appointed position, then I would.

Though still, even in private…the tears never really came.

But now that I have someone like Jax holding me and speaking to me in the least judgmental way…of course my body would try to betray me.

"M'fine." I clear my throat, pushing back from him before I can get myself too attached to his warmth. "You should go."

He nods, his eyes sullen with sadness. "If you can call me a cab, I'll meet it down at the gates."

Strangely enough, I hesitate.

I don't have time to read deeper into that before another knock at the office door is interrupting us. It has me rolling my eyes.

"What?"

"Ma'am, the other guests have begun arriving. Shall I send someone up to bring your guest to a room? We can arrange another place setting down at the table."

"Shit…" I mumble and run a hand through my hair.

That damn party… I forgot it was happening tonight.

"I can go…" Jax trails off, eyeing the door.

I shake my head at him before answering my butler. "Send someone up. No need for a place setting. I'll have someone bring him food to his room."

"Very well, ma'am. I'll get that notified through the staff."

"Thank you," I say before turning back to Jax.

My uncle had convinced me yesterday to have some of our more senior contracts over for a dinner in order to show them that the Devlins were still a force to be reckoned with. The death of our matron wouldn't be shaking our foundation, and I was already trained as a proper shoe-in for the position.

It was a smart suggestion on my uncle's part, but

now that the occasion is here, I want to do anything but go downstairs and shmooze.

"Listen to me." I jab Jax in the chest with a finger. "You're going to behave and stay in your room until I can get you a cab in the morning, do you understand me? Once the sun is up, I expect your bags to be packed and you ready to get off my property and back to America where you belong."

Jax stares at me for a long moment. "Amelia… would it kill you to be even a little happy to see me?"

I know by that ironic tone that he's teasing me—and oddly enough, I want to give into it a little bit—but I don't have time for this. I need him out of my hair before I can get myself distracted again. He's wonderful for that and not something I need in my life right now with everything practically hanging in the balance of one wrong move.

"Jax," I speak slowly. "You're leaving in the morning. Is that clear?"

He sighs. "Yeah, fine. All right."

"Good." My hands fist the front of his shirt in a tight grip.

He stumbles slightly as I yank him over to the door, opening it and shoving him out into the hallway. He huffs at me and rights himself, giving me a small glare that has me smiling despite myself.

"Really?" he says, fixing the strap of his bag over his shoulder.

Right as I'm about to say something back, one of

the maids comes heading down the hall for us. “Miss Amelia, is this the guest I’m escorting?”

“Yes. Take him to the east quarters.”

“Of course, ma’am.”

I lean against the doorway as Jax is led down the hall and to the opposite side of the mansion from me. Maybe it’s a little overkill, keeping him so far away from me, but hopefully that’ll keep him from tempting me into doing something stupid.

Hopefully.

CHAPTER 19

Jax

By the time the sun sets outside of my window, I'm already going completely stir crazy.

With a phone that hasn't been set up for this country's towers yet, along with a guard stationed outside of my room, I'm all but trapped in here until the morning. Not that I never took Amelia's threats to me seriously, but it feels like overkill.

Though, judging by the insane magnitude of this mansion, maybe it was safe to say whatever her and her family were involved in was a lot bigger than simply "old money." When I'd been left at the front gates, the two men that had questioned me on my reasonings for being there both had visible guns strapped to their waistbands and looked big enough to crush me.

Even when I'd finally be escorted up to the property, there had been more men with guns that greeted us on the front steps, along with more that were inside that put my bag through a scanner to check for any weapons.

All of it seemed to me like whatever Amelia's family was involved in was big enough to warrant that kind of suspiciousness of outside guests.

Since my window is facing outside toward the opposite end of the mansion and away from the drive leading up from the road, I have no idea how many people, or guests as her butler had specified, were coming here.

Though I suspect that even if I did know, I'd have no idea what for.

With nothing left to do but go to sleep, I fall back onto my bed and stare up at the ceiling. The room she's put me up in is nice, reminding me of a hotel room actually. It's fully furnished with a king-size bed, along with a small sitting area over by the windows. There's also a small bathroom attached as well.

All in all, it's quite the accommodation considering I pretty much barged in unannounced.

I wonder what Amelia had been thinking when she saw me. She certainly looked shocked… Was she upset I came all this way to check up on her or was it more at the inconvenience of housing me without warning? To me, she struck me as the type to always plan for everything, so someone like me coming over unannounced was more than likely a giant roadblock in her way.

I want to apologize, but I have a sneaking suspicion she's not going to be around tomorrow morning when I'm fetched and collected. I also wouldn't be surprised if she had guards follow me all the way onto the plane to make sure I got on it.

It makes me sad because all I want to do is talk to her. Even if it's for five minutes. I've grown so attached to her that our simple hug had left my heart pounding.

Across the room, I hear voices outside my door.

Sitting up, I blink into the darkness as shadows under the doorway move. It sounds like arguing, but I can't really make out what anyone's saying. Before I can slip off the bed and head over to the door to eavesdrop, it's already opening.

My eyes wince at the sudden shift in light, blink a few times as I try to clear my vision. Amelia stands in the doorway, dressed in a gown that reaches the floor and has a slit up the leg that goes all the way up to her hip.

Her hair is down in long bouncy curls, and she has dark eye makeup on that brings out the sharp features of her face.

She looks incredible as always.

Behind her, the guard that's been posted outside of my door shifts nervously. Before he has a chance to say anything else, Amelia turns and slams the door in his face, plunging the room into darkness again.

She makes a noise that sounds close to annoyed,

and I hear the sounds of her patting the wall until she finds the light switch to flick on. I blink again, adjusting to the light overhead before looking back at her.

"Hey…"

She frowns at me and stumbles slightly as she walks over to me. "You…"

I slide off the bed and head over to her, catching her as she stumbles again. I can smell the alcohol wafting off of her, overpouring over her lightly scented perfume. Not taking a second to think about it, I bend and scoop her up into my arms, ignoring the surprised grunt out of her mouth before bringing her over to the bed.

Setting her down gently, I drop to my knees in front of her and grab her by the ankle. I slip my fingers along her skin, finding the clasp of her heel and tugging it from around her ankle before slipping her shoe off completely. I do that to the other side before keeping her foot in my grasp and moving my fingers along the arch of her foot.

Amelia leans back on her hands and groans, her toes flexing as I massage the sore muscles. "Damn… you're…always s'good with your hands…"

I smile at the compliment. "How was the party?"

"Fucking annoying." Her words aren't as slurred as the alcohol scent coming off of her would suggest, which I suppose is a good thing. "I hate all those pricks… All of 'em think I'm not cut out for this…"

Arching my brow, I dig my fingers into the

bridge of her foot, earning another groan. "What job?"

"Running my family's business."

Family business? For some reason, I don't exactly believe her. Not with the size of this damn mansion and with her wild disguises that she'd donned when I first met her. There has to be more to her "work life" that I'm missing. There is old money here for sure, but something else too.

"And," I switch to the other foot while speaking, "what's the family business?"

She scoffs at me but then sighs, closing her eyes. "Guns mostly. Sometimes other stuff…depends…"

My hands pause for a second. "…Guns?"

"Mmm." She wiggles her toes at me expectantly.

Quickly, I go back to moving them along the bottoms of her feet. Guns? Why the hell would she be dealing with guns? Only gang members deal with that kind of—

My eyes go wide. "…Amelia."

"Hm."

Slowly, I look up at her. "Are…you in a gang?"

She breathes out a laugh. "Mafia. That's the word you're looking for."

My mouth drops open. I watch as she leans back and flops down onto my mattress, sighing softly to herself. Letting go of her foot, I stand slowly and look over her. She looks content laying on my bed with her beautiful red hair spread out all around her.

Why hadn't I seen this before? All the suspicious

activities with covering up her identity, always bringing me back to her hotel room, the metal card, the way Neil had gotten freaked out when he saw it, the goddamn mega mansion I'd been brought to, the guards upon *guards* littering the place.

Jesus, it was all right in front of me, and yet I'm still standing here shocked beyond belief.

Amelia Devlin is the current mafia head of her family.

It suits her, and yet I still find it so hard to believe that I'm in the presence of someone so powerful.

Her body relaxes more, her face going slack as sleep takes her. Affection thumps inside of my chest, a smile crossing over my face as I hear her breathing deepen. As carefully as I can, I grab her legs and carefully move her further onto the bed.

Thankfully my covers were already tucked back from before, so it's easy for me to pull them over her and get her cozy.

She grunts at me, her eyes fluttering open while a scowl tugs down at her lips. "Jax..."

"Yes?"

"The fuck."

My hand hesitates, still gripping the covers. "What?"

"Get me out of this thing..."

She shoves the covers back, yanking them out of my hand, and then sits up with another grunt. Oh, her dress, I realize as she cranes her hand back to try and grab at the zipper. Crawling onto the bed behind her, I catch the zipper and pull it down slowly, revealing creamy white skin underneath.

She wiggles out of her dress, helping me by laying down again and lifting her hips so I can shimmy it off of her. The second she's naked and free, she rolls back onto her back and lets out a sigh of relief.

"Better?" I ask, tossing her dress onto the floor.

Maybe I should hang it up, but I don't want to leave her for even a second, not when she's laying in my bed naked and beautiful.

"Mhmm." Her eyes slide shut again.

Grabbing the covers again, I slide in next to her and pull them over us. It's weird how comfortable I am with Amelia sleeping next to me, even with the revelation that she's a fucking mafia...princess? Queen? I don't even know what the proper terms for it are.

I've never met anyone from a mafia family, let alone got involved with one.

But Amelia's so different. She's nothing like I've ever expected, and I think that's why my brain has latched onto her like it has. She's everything that a strong and capable woman is, she doesn't take shit from anyone, and she's not afraid to put people in their place.

I admire her for it, in fact.

Reaching over, I gently tuck a few pieces of her

hair away from her face and lie on my side to face her. Her breathing has already grown slow, sleeping taking her immediately.

While I watch her sleep, I wonder what she dreams of.

CHAPTER 20

Amelia

WAKING UP, I feel enveloped in warmth.

It's the first time in an entire week that I've felt comfortable and not like the weight of immediate dread is crushing me to death. I want to lay here and stay in this wonderful feeling until I can't anymore, let my body finally relax after everything I've been forcing myself to be put through.

Slowly opening my eyes, I notice that it's not a blanket that's covering me and keeping me warm, but a pair of arms. I follow them up, finding the curve of a shoulder and then a neck until I realize that I'm quite literally buried in Jax's arms.

It has me snorting to myself.

In all of the times we'd slept together, I never took him as a cuddler. Then again, I was always up and gone before he had a real chance of worming his way over to my side of the bed. I can't say I hate it, though. In fact…it feels rather nice after feeling the blood in my veins turn to ice the moment I learned of my mother's death.

My heart still aches, but this morning, it's a dull pain.

Running my hand up Jax's back, I can map the planes of his hard muscles under the thin t-shirt he's wearing. They feel nice, even when they're not flexed; it makes me want to dig my nails into them and scratch angry red lines down the unmarred skin underneath.

My other hand wanders in the opposite direction, feeling for where his thigh is pressed against me and then dipping around it to find the waistband of his sweats. A slow breath tickles my neck when I slip my hand under the waistband and trail over the small patch of soft hair at the base of his cock.

It's soft in my hand but hardens almost immediately as I grip it, stroking slowly and running my thumb along the head of it. Jax's arms tighten around me, his body moving slightly in order to make room for me to scootch in and get a better angle. I can tell by the way that he's breathing that he's still asleep, but whatever he's dreaming around is turning him on.

His hips move slightly, his cock grinding against my hand as I stroke it from the base to the tip, teasing him by changing the pressure of my fingers around him. A soft groan leaves his lips, causing me to smile.

Oh, I love how desperate he gets. It really is such a turn-on.

Using my shoulder, I wiggle out from under him and push him onto his back, slipping my hand out from under his sweats to do so. His body stretches out, legs moving apart while one of his arms comes up to cover his face. He relaxes again soon after that, falling back into his dreams once more.

When I sit up, I grab at his sweats and pull them down past his hips, exposing his cock to me. He bounces against his stomach, the head of it already drooling with precum from me touching it. I grip it again and run my fingers along the tip, smearing it all over before dragging my hand back down.

Jax lets out another groan, satisfying me. I'm already wet between my legs and ready to straddle him at any second, but for now, I kind of like to watch him struggle. He's powerless under my hands, even when he's awake. He loves it when I take control and show him who he belongs to.

The thought strikes me suddenly. *Where did* that *come from?*

Shaking my head, I ignore it and let go of him in order to put my hands on his chest to steady myself as I swing a leg over and straddle him. He feels perfect, slipping between my pussy lips, his cockhead still oozing with cum. As much as I want to get him off and drizzle all that on his stomach, I'd much prefer him filling me up with it instead.

Grabbing him again, I line the head up with my

hole and bear down onto it. A surprised gasp leaves me, his thick cock stretching me as I slide down onto him. Fuck, I missed this way too much. He really has the perfect cock to fuck—it's like my very own personalized dildo made just for me in all the ways I like.

As soon as my hips are pressed flushed to his, I settle on him for a second. Leaning over, I grab his arm and push it off of his face, revealing his flushed cheeks and slightly parted lips. He's never looked so damn good in his life.

I roll my hips along his, moving him slightly inside of me but not enough to actually go anywhere. It feels good, though, with my clit rubbing against the base of his cock like this, him filling me almost to the point where it hurts. I love it —having sex with Jax is always a good experience.

Putting my hands on his chest, I finally lift myself up before slamming back down onto him. It has me moaning; the sounds of my wet pussy moving up and down on him sounds almost obscene. I'm so fucking wet for him, though, that some of my slick drizzles down onto his skin, wetting it slightly.

"Fuck," I mumble and throw my head back, fucking myself on him like my favorite sex toy.

God, I love it. I could do this all fucking day. He really has the perfect cock. It fills me just right and rubs against every single sensitive nerve I have inside of me. Leaning my head back, I watch as his lips part and his face flushes even more.

His eyes flutter open. "Oh fuck, you really are here."

I smirk down at him. "Dreaming about me?"

Instead of answering me, though, he reaches up and grabs my hips, holding them in a tight grip as he slams up into me to meet my own rocking motions. It has me gasping out in pleasure, my entire body practically rocketing off of the bed from how good it feels.

If I could keep him chained to my bed all day, I would.

Actually, that's not a bad arrangement.

"Oh fuck, Amelia," he says to me, his eyes wide and desperate. "I'm gonna come."

My pussy clenches tighter around him, already ready to milk him fucking dry. "Do it, come in me."

As if my permission alone got him off, Jax's back arches. His thrusting becomes desperate, pounding into me hard enough to shock me into my own orgasm. I choke out a moan, my thighs shaking from the effort of having to hold myself up. Jax's thrusts become erratic, chasing his own pleasure as my pussy squeezes his cock in a vice grip.

He comes with a long groan, pressing up into me as far as he can until he's bathing my insides with his cum. I shudder, digging my nails into his skin to keep myself from falling over on top of him. His chest is moving rapidly under my hands, panting as he shallowly thrusts into me one more time before dropping back down onto the bed and going still.

His skin has a fine sheen of sweat on it, giving him a dewy look. "Good morning…"

I smile. "Morning."

"That was a nice way to wake up."

"Mmm, I bet."

Honestly, it's the *only* way to wake up in my opinion. Who doesn't want to get laid first thing in the morning?

Leaning over, I prop my hips up and let him slide out of me. Cum comes spilling out almost immediately, coating his lower belly in both of our fluids. He scoffs at me, giving me a "really?" look as I simply grin.

What can I say? I like to share.

I swing my leg over and roll off of him, my body already feeling amazing since I got such great sleep last night. It was partially because of the alcohol and partially due to Jax, so I suppose I have both to thank.

Out of the corner of my eye, I see him sit up slowly. "Where are you going?"

"Unlike you, I have a job to do," I say, bending to grab my dress and slip it on without zipping it up.

While my own bedroom is across the other side of the mansion, I don't exactly mind walking around half dressed. Hardly any of my guests from last night stayed, and the ones who did I knew would not be getting up until well after noon judging by how much they drank last night.

Turning to him, I give him a wink. “Bathroom should be stocked.”

He scoffs at me again. “Seriously?”

I simply laugh and heave over to the door, not bothering to quip back with anything else. And with that, I leave.

CHAPTER 21

Jax

I DON'T GET HER.

I really don't.

Running my hands through my freshly washed hair, I pace around my room for what feels like an hour. The morning comes and goes, and to my surprise, no one comes to collect me to leave. Instead, what *does* end up happening is me getting invited downstairs for breakfast.

I'm not expecting it at all when one of the maids comes around knocking on my door, but the second she tells me that I'm expected down at breakfast, I drop my bags and follow her.

There's no one else down here besides me and a few of the other waitstaff, something that I'm kind of grateful for. I have no idea how I would go about explaining myself to any of Amelia's guests of family members about our relationship or how we know each other, and I doubted Amelia wanted anyone to know that I was privy to the fact that this was a damn mafia family.

Still, confusion clouds my head.

Digging into my breakfast, I practically moan at the taste. It's actually divine and the best thing I've had in what feels like forever.

"Jackson?"

My eyes snap up from my plate.

At first, I don't see where the voice is coming from, but then out of the corner of my eye, I see movement. Turning toward it, I see a small door closing and a man, close to my age, walking over toward the table.

Blinking a few times in surprise, I say, "Aidan…?"

He smiles. "Fancy seeing you here."

I can't help but stare at the man as he sits down across from me at the table. He leans back when one of the waitstaff comes over and puts a plate of food in front of him, his fingers nimbly grabbing his silverware off of the cloth napkin next to his hand and unfolding it before placing it in his lap.

When he looks up at me again, he raises a brow. "Amelia mentioned you were here."

How…how the hell…?

Aidan O'Conner was the last person on this planet that I would've ever guessed would be sitting across from me eating breakfast in the middle of a goddamn mafia house. We'd gone to college together, both of us studying law and bemoaning our fates while we studied together for the LSATS. It had been a horrible year, but we'd both made it, forced to be separated once his student visa was up and he headed back to Europe.

I had no idea this is where he ended up, though.

"You know Amelia…" is the first thing that comes out of my mouth.

"Well, yes. I am currently living in her family's estate."

Inwardly, I roll my eyes. That much is obvious.

"I meant…*how* do you know Amelia?"

He smiles at me, his shrewd eyes watching me as he forks a piece of potato into his mouth before answering me. "Shouldn't I be asking *you* that?"

Ugh, good point…

"We were acquainted back in the States. She was over there for business."

"Hm. I don't remember her mentioning getting into any legal trouble over there."

He's obviously digging for the real reason, which leads me to assume that Amelia didn't give him any details other than me simply being here. I'm not sure how much I'm supposed to divulge anyways, seeing as I was supposed to leave early this morning but haven't.

Is she keeping me for a reason? Maybe the lay had been good enough for her to reconsider sending me packing.

As much as that should be insulting, it actually makes me happy. Giving her that kind of pleasure, enough for her to keep me around for a little while longer, hits me deep in my chest.

"She isn't—or wasn't, I mean. We got acquainted for personal reasons. I came over to check up on her after she left."

"Ah." Aidan nods slowly, forking some of his egg. "Yes, it has been such a tragedy."

I study him, trying to figure out how best to ask *what* happened without making it too obvious that I don't know. I doubt Aidan will tell me anything if Amelia hasn't already expressed to him that she wants him to. How far their relationship goes is a mystery, but from what I know of Amelia, she doesn't trust easily.

Which leads me to believe that Aidan is someone important to her if she's told him about me being here.

"Aidan." I lean forward. "Are you...part of all of this?"

He raises a brow at me, a piece of his sandy-colored hair falling over one of his eyes to block it from view. "A part of what?"

"This...family business."

It's awkward coming out of my mouth, but I don't know how insulting it is for people to go around calling others mafia gang members. It's not like Amelia gave me a crash course in how to navigate these things. Hell—we hadn't exactly done a lot of talking this morning, anyway.

Aidan huffs out a laugh. "Yes. Isn't that obvious by me being here?"

"I didn't figure you for, uh…" I wave my hand in the air, not knowing how to finish the sentence.

"What, mafia?" He shrugs at me, leaning back in his chair. "Well, it is a family business, after all."

"So are you and Amelia related?"

"No. But I do work for her."

Interesting… In the two years that Aidan and I were friends in college, not once did he ever give me the impression that he or his family worked for an illegal business. He talked about his home life pretty often, mentioning his overbearing dad and his mother that died into his early teen years.

But nothing of the sort would've had me guessing that he was bred into the mafia.

"I see…"

Amusement tickles his eyes. "Do you? It seems to me like you're rather lost."

I sigh. Always so shrewd. That's what I always used to appreciate about having him as my study partner; he could pick out the fine details in things that would otherwise go completely missed. Now that it's been turned around on me, though, I'm beginning to see why everyone hated debating against us.

"Look, I'll admit, I have no idea what I've gotten myself into. But I care about Amelia, and I want her to be safe and well taken care of, that's all."

"That's mighty noble of you."

Is it? It seems like I'm simply being a decent human being.

"I guess. Do you not care about her?"

"Oh, I do. I am her liaison, after all."

That has me blinking in surprise. "You are?"

"Yes. For now." He smiles again, lifting his fork to his mouth. "Will you also be joining us for a time?"

"I'm not sure. I'm here till Amelia kicks me out."

That has him laughing. "I see. Hopefully you'll be staying more than a day."

Yeah, not likely...

"Hopefully," is what I say back.

I finish my food while my head swims.

"Aidan, tell me something."

He lifts his eyes up from his plate. "Hm?"

I pause, rolling the words around in my head before speaking them out loud. "Is she going to be okay?"

He pauses as well, seeming to think over his own before answering me. "She will be."

THOSE WORDS SEEM to haunt me, even as I'm escorted back to my room.

I can't imagine what Amelia's going through, but clearly whatever it is, everyone knows about it. I can't say for sure that Aidan had looked worried per se, but there was definitely a tinge of concern in his eyes that made the pit in my stomach tighten.

Seeing Amelia look so tired when I'd seen her in her office had been a shock. Even though I should've been expecting it considering her abrupt departure, I still wasn't prepared for how sad and worn out she was.

I wish she'd let me stay and help her. I'd do whatever she wanted if only she asked.

Looking up from where I'd been staring off into space as we walked, I notice that we're not in the same hallway we were when I'd been brought down for breakfast. Instead, I recognize this as the same hallway to where Amelia's office is.

My heart picks up while I silently follow the guard a few paces behind him.

He stands in front of a familiar door, knocking twice before waiting for Amelia to answer him, and then opens it. "I have your guest?"

"Send him in," I hear her say.

The guard steps back, sweeping his hand around to motion me to enter. Heading around the doorway, I step inside of Amelia's office.

I never got a good look at it yesterday when I was in here—much too busy focusing on Amelia and how much I truly missed her to notice anything—but now that I am, I realize this office is gigantic.

There is enough room for not only a sitting area in the center of the room but a small mini bar for entertaining too. At the back wall are large windows that overlook some kind of garden as well as a long wood desk and chair set in front of it, facing out toward the office space.

Amelia isn't sitting at the desk but rather in the armchair where the seating area is. Across from her is a man that looks around sixty, his bald head shiny in the natural lighting coming from the windows.

When the door closes behind me, both Amelia and the man turn to stare at me.

"Ah, this must be the lawyer you were talking about." the man smiles.

...What?

Glancing over at Amelia quickly, I notice she's giving me a hard stare. Clearing my throat, I head over and hold out my hand. "Jackson Baxter. It's nice to meet you."

The firm grip on my hand tells me everything I need to know about this man. "Sean Devlin. I'm Amelia's uncle."

Ah, an actual family member.

While I don't quite see the resemblance, I can tell he's got that same sort of energy that exudes from Amelia.

Once Sean lets go of my hand, I move over to the other couch across from him and lean back into it. I have no fucking clue what Amelia's plan is here, but if she wants to play it like I'm her lawyer, then I'm her damn lawyer, no questions asked.

"Please," I hold my hands up, crossing my leg over my knee. "Carry on."

Amelia's lip quirks up slightly before she quickly

stifles it. “We were just going over my mother’s assets. As the next living heir, I’ll be entitled to all of them, including her contracts.”

The gears in my head start spinning. Is that what happened? He mother passed? If that’s the case, then I feel horrible for her. I know what it’s like to lose a parent, especially so unexpectedly. If she truly had lost her mother while she’d been out with me, then I could understand why she completely cut everything and ran back home to be with her family.

If that happened to me, I’d do whatever it took to get back to my sister. You needed family to lean on when someone important like that passed; it was too devastating to bear without that kind of support system.

“Well, not all contracts,” her uncle corrected. “There are still a few that need to be sorted out.”

Amelia gestures to me. “That’s why I’ve brought him on. He’ll be able to go through them in no time and sort out what needs to be done in order to retain them.”

While I love her confidence in me, I’m not all that well versed in business contracts. My area of expertise was criminal law and prosecuting businesses who conducted illegal practices. I’d have to refresh myself on contractual agreements if I wanted to help Amelia—especially Irish ones.

Because that was a whole different ball game.

Her uncle frowns, slightly moving in his seat.

"Amelia…while I appreciate the confidence, these things take time."

Her cool expression practically gives me frostbite. "I'm not interested in that. I want it done, and that's what Jax is here to do. To get it done. We don't have time to waste with the O'Conners already breathing down our necks."

Wait, O'Conners? As in Aidan's family?

Sean sighs. "Yes, well. I'm sure that has *nothing* to do with you scooping up their only heir and hiding him out here."

"I'm not hiding him out anywhere. He chooses to live here. It isn't like his father doesn't know he's here."

"I'm sure he believes him to be a spy."

"I doubt that," Amelia argues back. "It doesn't matter what the cause is. What matters is the outcome. I'm not going to let the O'Conners get it in their heads that they've got the balls to take on us Devlins. It's not happening."

"Let me talk to them."

Amelia shakes her head before standing. "I'm done trying to negotiate. They've already shown how two-faced they can be before any of this started. I'm not about to let them try and weasel their way back into our good graces just because they think they can hit us while we're grieving."

Sean sighs again. "If that's what you insist."

"It is. We're done talking about this."

He chuckles, looking over at me. "Good luck with her. She's quite the handful."

For some reason, his tone has me frowning. He's smiling as he says it, but something in his eyes feels off to me. I can't quite put my finger on it, but I don't like it.

Instead of agreeing with him, I simply stare back, not wanting to give him any sort of satisfaction for trying to disrespect Amelia like this.

Sean shakes his head and pushes up from his thighs to stand. "Amelia, please let me know where you get with those contracts. I'd like to look them over before you send them out."

"I'll try."

I follow him as he crosses the office over to the door. He glances back at me to nod and say, "It was nice meeting you, Jackson. I'm sure we'll be seeing more of each other very soon."

I give him a returning nod, waiting until he's out the door and the jam has clicked back into place before turning to face Amelia. She's already over by her desk, her back to me as she sorts through the mess of papers on top of it.

Getting up, I head over to her. "Amelia."

"What?"

I stop just before my body collides with her. "Were you actually serious about me helping you?"

I hope to hell she says yes and that this isn't all some ploy to tug at my heartstrings.

She sighs, her head sinking down while she rubs her hands over her face. "No. Not really…"

I can sense a "but" in there, and it has me reaching out to grab her by her shoulders and spin her around. I pull her hands away from her face and cup her cheeks in order to tilt her head back up to look at me.

"Let me help you."

She frowns but doesn't say anything.

"I promise, I can be useful in and outside of the bedroom."

Her lip quirks slightly. "How multifaceted of you."

My fingers squeeze her jaw. "Please. I've got a visa until the end of the month. At least let me help you get started on whatever it is you need to go through for your contracts."

I watch her hesitate as she contemplates my offer. I can tell her first instinct is to tell me no, but logic is outweighing her. Judging by the mounds of paperwork stacked up behind her, it's obvious that she's overwhelmed. If she's the only one going through any of this stuff, I can imagine how tired she really is, despite that brave face she put on.

Not to mention she's grieving her mother on top of that.

The thought saddens me. "I'm sorry."

Her brows furrow together. "About?"

Leaning down, I brush my lips over hers, pulling her into a gentle kiss. She surprises me but sags into me slightly, her hands coming up to grab onto my biceps as I tilt our mouths to deepen the kiss.

When I finally pull back, I say, "For your mother."

She sighs again. "Yeah..."

"It's hard to lose a parent."

She gives me a rather sardonic smile. "Sounds like you have experience."

"Unfortunately."

Amelia pulls away from me completely then, running her hands over her face. "I just want to be done with all of this. The old laws are already working against me being a woman. I don't need any more shit piled onto my plate to keep me distracted."

Nodding, I cup her face again. I don't want to let her go—I'm too addicted to touching her. I want to make her feel better in any way that I can, even if it's just something small like running my thumb over her cheek.

"Let me help you then. It will take some stress off your plate. Besides, I'll know where to look to gather information much faster than you can. Use me for the month you have me."

It's silly to be begging this much in order to stay, but I can't help it. I'm addicted to her, and the thought of being forced to leave kind of kills me.

Finally, Amelia looks up at me with those deep green eyes of hers and says, "All right."

CHAPTER 22

Jax

For the first week, everything goes rather smoothly.

Amelia and I have a pretty symbiotic working relationship that I never would've expected. Not only is she forward with what she wants—something that I love in a client—but she's open about the "rules" that her family typically abides by.

Which is almost none.

Still, there is a certain code that the mafia works under that I can appreciate, so while it may freak me out a little that I'm currently helping people skirt under the law for personal gain, it also doesn't feel like I'm betraying my moral compass.

At least not horribly.

Not enough for me to completely contemplate my entire moral compass.

Either way, though, I enjoy what I'm doing with Amelia so far.

The more I spend time with her, the more I can feel myself growing comfortable with her in a way I've never felt with anyone before. Of course, the sex is fantastic, but besides that, we are able to talk to each other for hours, it seems, once we've turned in for the night.

I don't know how it started, but around the end of the first week, I'd gone back to Amelia's room and hadn't left since.

Which is absolutely not something I was complaining about in the slightest.

Amelia also seemed to be warming up to me too, even going so far as to tell me what it was like growing up with her mother and later telling me about the tragic death of her father and brother.

"Honestly, no one expected it," she'd said one night, curled up on her side facing me. "They were here one minute and gone the next. There was barely anything left of them from what the coroner told us. I guess the semi that hit them was going over eighty."

"Jesus," I breathed out. "Amelia...I'm so sorry."

She shrugged at me in the darkness, my eyes barely able to pick it up. "Ever since then it was just me and my mom. I wish I got to say goodbye to her before..."

She'd choked up then, not wanting to continue, and for that reason, I never pushed her.

I didn't want her to feel obligated to tell me, especially since whatever is brewing between us seems so fragile and easily severed anyway. I want this relationship to have some kind of fighting chance, even if it seems like I'm the only one wanting it to be more than us just fucking.

Call me a romantic at heart, but I can see myself staying here with Amelia for a while. Even after my month's visa is up. How I'll go about doing that is anyone's guess, but there are always loopholes.

By the time the second week rolls around, though, I start to feel something fishy brewing around the mansion.

It starts out with small things like walking past certain people and their conversations stopping once I reached them or passed by. Or something as innocuous as the waitstaff giving Amelia and me looks as we dined together for our meals, Aidan occasionally joining us for them.

All of it had been starting to make me feel strangely, and that part of my brain that I could never shut off, the one that is always so highly suspicious of everyone, couldn't help but nag at me over and over again.

It wasn't until I finally caught the conversation of a few of the maids changing out the sheets to my old room that I finally got my first piece of information.

"Did you hear Miss Amelia is going to approach the O'Conners soon?" one of them says.

"I heard. But you know how Mr. Sean feels about that," another one chimes in.

I lean my back against the wall, pressing myself

into it while the maids just across the corner continue on. I'd only been walking back from grabbing some bottles of water from the kitchen before heading back to Amelia's office when I'd noticed them all.

Is it morally wrong to spy on people? Sure, but not when it could come down to something fishy going on behind Amelia's back.

"You think he's going to do something about it?" one of them asks.

"I heard that Mr. Sean was pretty upset when Miss Amelia came back. I think he was planning on taking over the business."

One of the maids gasps. "Really?"

"Mhmmm."

"Do you think he'll try to do something?"

"Like what? That's his niece."

"True…"

"He's an opportunistic man. I'm sure he'll find something else he can control that suits him."

I frown as they all head off further down the hall, their conversation carrying with them. Sean wanting to usurp Amelia? That didn't sound good. But it makes sense as to why I was getting a bad vibe from him when we first met.

It wasn't that he'd been unfriendly, but there had been a coldness to his eyes that I hadn't been expecting. Not when someone's tone of voice and smile led you to believe he was by far the opposite.

Still, it didn't bode well. Even if he wasn't trying

to do anything to sabotage Amelia, I didn't like someone like that being around her. Resentment could lead to people doing horrible things—to which I'd seen firsthand in my career too many times to count.

As long as someone like that was running around the halls of this mansion unchecked, we would have a problem.

Heading back to Amelia's office, I adjust the water bottles in my hands before grabbing onto the handle to the door. On the other side of the thick door, I can hear the distinct voices of someone shouting.

With my heart hammering, I shove the door open, letting it bang against the opposite wall. Both Amelia and her uncle spin around to me, their faces flushed from yelling at each other.

"What is going on?" I demand.

Sean is the first to pull himself together. "Nothing. Amelia and I were just discussing some things. Family things," he clarifies.

She glares at him. "I think we're done here."

"Amelia—"

"We're. Done," she spits out. "Jax and I have things to do. So if you don't mind."

With a sweeping gesture, she motions for the door.

Sean stands rooted to his spot for a moment longer before finally shaking his head and heading out of the office. As he passes me, his eyes gaze over, regarding me with a cool look before he grabs the door and shuts it behind him.

I stare back at it for a long moment before turning back to Amelia. "What the hell was that?"

She sighs before collapsing onto the couch. "He wants to force the O'Conners' hand."

"Why?" I ask, heading over to her and handing her one of the water bottles.

"Who knows? He thinks that by doing so, it will show our strength, but all it's really going to do is get people unnecessarily killed."

True…not to mention there's no guarantee what the outcome will be. For all Sean knew, it could mean the end of their empire.

"What are you going to do?" I ask.

She cracks open the water bottle, draining half of it before speaking again. "I want us to keep doing what we're doing. As long as we get these contracts figured out, everything else will fall into place."

I can't help but latch onto the word *us*.

It makes me smile. Maybe she'll keep me after all.

"Sounds good to me. Where would you like to start today?"

"Let's start combing through our overseas contracts."

"You got it."

ONCE EVENING HITS, I feel exhaustion hit me like a ton of bricks.

Across from me on the opposite couch, Amelia raises her arms above her head and yawns as well.

The gesture has me smiling. "Want to call it a night?"

She grunts at me, rubbing at her eyes. "We probably should. My eyes are burning."

I set down the stack of papers in my lap and stand, feeling practically all of my bones crack back into place. I hold out my hand to her, pulling her up once she takes it. I don't let her slip her hand away from mine and instead lace our fingers together.

She looks down at them with bleary eyes, shrugging to herself before using our laced fingers to tug me over to the door. I follow after her willingly, not bothering to suggest we pick up her office before heading out. The mess will be there tomorrow, anyway, and I'm sure we'll make more of it.

Amelia leads me down the hall to her room where she strips bare and tugs at my clothes until I do the same. Wordlessly, she grabs my hand again and pulls me toward the bed, pushing me down onto it before hopping up herself.

I'm so tired, but if she wants to fuck me, I'll gladly go along with it. I'd never pass up an opportunity to have that incredible wet heat wrapped around me.

She surprises me though by ripping the covers back from under me before crawling on top of me and laying down. Using her free hand, she tugs the covers over us and then rests her head against my chest, letting out a content sigh.

It has me blinking down at her.

What...the hell?

My heart thunders in my chest, embarrassing me. Her ear must pick up on it because she snorts and then tucks an arm around my waist. Her lashes tickle my skin as they flutter closed, her body becoming lax as she quickly drifts off to sleep.

I never…expected her to make a move like this. Usually it's me rolling over in my sleep and pulling her into a tight hold that we both wake up from and fuck out of. It's never Amelia who initiates these intimate contacts with me.

My entire body hums with a warm glow.

God, I could really get used to this.

I hope she lets me.

CHAPTER 23

Jax

THE MORNING SUN wakes me slowly.

As I stretch and roll onto my side, I dimly notice how cold the other side of the bed is. Patting it, I feel the sudden absence of Amelia, my heart sinking a little. I know she's most likely in her office working, but I'm sad she hasn't decided to get up with me today.

Since falling into a sort of routine with her over the past few days, I'd gotten used to waking up with her still sleeping on my chest, exhausted from spending hours poring over the seemingly never-ending paperwork. I'm glad that she had least had me to buffer some of it, though.

The deeper we got into what had really been going on in the Devlin estate, the more we were both steadily realizing how messy it all was. To me, it seemed that Amelia's mother had been trying to keep the entire organization from crumbling due to her uncle's poor financial decisions in the past.

I wasn't sure how far back these blunders had gone, but it was safe to say that if the Devlin family was ever entrusted to Sean, it would result in a complete nightmare of ruin. Thankfully, Amelia had been steadfast in her pursuit of keeping the man at bay while also moving in the shadows in order to continue to bridge her mother's old contracts to becoming her own.

As I watched her grow into this new role, I really had to say, I was proud of her. It was clear to me that she was incredibly dedicated to taking care of her family the way they needed to be as well as not taking any shit from those that were threatening that tight hold she had on them.

Wherever this path was leading her, she was meant for it.

Getting up, I stretch again and slide the covers off of myself. There's a slight chill in the air that has my skin pinprickle as I swing my legs over the edge and stand. Pulling on some loose-fitting clothes, I head downstairs and spot a few of the waitstaff cleaning up breakfast with no one else aside from myself in sight.

"Good morning, Jax." One of them nods to me, an older woman that I've come to know as Shelly. "Shall we get you and Miss Amelia's breakfast ready?"

That has me raising a brow. "Amelia...hasn't come down for breakfast yet?"

“No. We figured you both were having a late morning.” There’s a twinkle in her eyes that I don’t miss—an amusement that’s rather suggestive.

I guess I shouldn’t be surprised that Amelia’s staff knows what’s going on between us. We hadn’t exactly been subtle…

“Uh…no.” I run my hand over my jaw. “Let me go grab her. I’m sure she’ll want to sit down before we get back into work.”

“Of course.” The woman smiles at me. “I’ll put a fresh pot of coffee on.”

“Thank you,” I tell her as I turn around and head out of the dining area.

That’s strange, Amelia’s never one to skip breakfast—especially since she’s been living off of coffee lately. I figured she’d already gone to her office to work, but it’s unexpected that she’d completely disregard anything else altogether.

Maybe she’s worried about something. Yesterday when we were going through the financial statements, she’d been a little off-put. The Devlins weren’t in debt by any means, but with Sean breathing down Amelia’s neck over the O’Conner situation, coupled with his past transgressions against the family, I would see why Amelia would be feeling restless.

As I head up the stairs to the other side of the mansion, I spot Aidan coming out of his room with his sandy-colored hair slightly messy and a pair of sweats loosely tied around his waist. The image of him—usually dressed so prim and proper—was kind of funny and reminded me of when we used to go out and party all night and then regret it after our eight a.m. class rolled around the next day.

"Long night?" I ask him as I approach him.

He rubs at his eyes. "Unfortunately. I got a call from Amelia this morning but missed it. I was coming down to see what she needed."

"Oh. You know what it was about?"

He shakes his head, dropping his arm. "No, the voicemail was rather strange."

For some reason, I don't like the sound of that.

"Mind if I hear?"

Aidan shrugs and pulls his cell out of his pocket, tapping on the screen a few times before putting the voicemail on speaker.

There's muffled rustling on the other end, almost like Amelia accidentally dialed him inside of her pocket. It goes on for a few more seconds before there's another muffled sound, sounding close to what a squeaky door opening would. It's abruptly cut off with a beat of silence before the voicemail ends.

"Strange, right?" Aidan lowers his phone.

"Very..." I mumble. "I'm headed to her office now if you'd like to come with me."

Aidan looks me up and down. "She isn't with you? That's surprising."

That has me rolling my eyes. "Knock it off."

My shoulder knocks with his as I pass by him

and head further down the hall. It's not that I hate people pointing out the obvious, but I'm not sure if Amelia would like people pointing it out in general.

I have no idea how far her feelings go for me, and I'm not about to push her into telling me just yet. Riding out this…whatever it is is enough for me right now. It's not like I have much time left to do so, anyway.

As we get to Amelia's office, I knock twice. Aidan brushes my shoulder when he stands next to me, letting out a big yawn.

"What kept you up so late last night?" I ask him.

He shrugs. "Well, between you and me, I was trying to track Amelia's uncle last night."

My brow raises. "Why?"

"I'm not sure. I had a weird feeling about him the other day."

"Weird as in…?"

He shrugs at me, leaving it at that.

I glance back at the door, wondering why Amelia isn't answering. It's too early to have a meeting—or so I thought. Leaning forward, my ear presses to the door as I listen for any other sounds on the other side.

"It's soundproof," comes Aidan's helpful motif.

Rolling my eyes, I lean back and try the handle, surprised to find it unlocked. Pushing the door open, I step into the office and look around. No one seems to have been in here since late last night when Amelia and I called it a day. Our stacks of papers are still spread out all over the table between the couches and along the floor at the foot of them.

Over by the window, the shades are still drawn, giving the entire office a soft glow from the rising sun.

Aside from a lone lamp left on over by Amelia's desk, the entire place is deserted.

"Thought you said she was in here?" Aidan says over my shoulder.

Shaking my head, I step in further, looking around. "I thought she was. The kitchen staff said she didn't come down for breakfast, and she wasn't there when I woke up this morning."

"Hm." He steps past me and heads over to the desk, side-stepping the stacks of papers with surprisingly limber footing.

I follow in after him, letting the door shut behind me. Where the hell could she have gone?

It isn't like her to up and disappear without saying anything. Maybe she left me a text that I missed before leaving the room. It wasn't like I had been particularly concerned with my phone over the past few days with Amelia being by my side.

Other than updating my sister every other day, my contacts had been relatively dry.

"Oh fuck." Aidan stumbles back, hitting the wall behind the desk.

Spinning around, I see his eyes widen.

"What?" Hurrying over, I knock over a stack of papers, sending them flying across the floor. "Shit."

"I think that's blood."

"*What*?" I hiss, finally getting over to him.

Peering around the desk, my eyes snap down to where he's pointing.

There, on the carpet right behind the desk, is a dark stain in the shape of a blood pool. My heart pounds as I lean over it, my fingers twitching when they graze across the surface of the carpet, wetness coating my skin and causing me to cringe.

I raise it and hold my hand under the light; a deep ruby red is smeared over the pads of my fingers.

"What the fuck?" I choke out.

"Look." Aidan steps around me again, his hand gripping my shoulder in a tight grasp as he bends to fish something out from underneath the desk.

When he holds it up, my heart sinks immediately.

Amelia's gun.

CHAPTER 24

Amelia

I WAKE up in a dingy room that looks unfamiliar.

There's a pounding in the back of my head that screams every time I try to lift my head from the pillow that I'm lying on. My entire body feels like it's on fire, a familiar sensation that brings me back to that one time at a bar down in Dublin where I was roofied.

Moving my limbs is chore, but I manage to finally get myself up into a sitting position without one, falling over, and two, throwing up. Spots cloud my vision as I try to blink away the pain for the headache.

I have no idea where I am, and even as I get the dots out of my vision and have a look around, I don't recognize anything.

Whatever room this is, it's small with only a single window in it that's been covered with a thin sheet in order to block most of the sun out. It casts a dim, yellowy glow around the room, making the entire space feel hazy in a way.

Looking down at myself, I'm wearing some kind of robe, an outfit that I only vaguely remember putting on before heading down to breakfast.

What time is it?

Judging by the sun trying to come in from behind the curtain, it's mid-afternoon at least, if not later.

My memories are scattered from rolling out of bed and pulling myself out of Jax's arms, to putting on my robe and heading down to grab us both food before we started on a new set of documents to go over.

Lifting my hand to rub my forehead, I feel something tug at my wrist. Opening my eyes, I look down to see a shackle latched around my wrist with a chain that leads to somewhere under the bed I'm sitting on.

...What the fuck?

Across the way, a door opens, letting in artificial light. "Ah, good. You're awake."

My heart picks up speed at the voice. "Uncle?"

He shuts the door behind him, walking over at a lazy speed that suddenly has my blood boiling. If this is some kind of elaborate way to convince me to try and dismantle the O'Conners, I'm going to lose my fucking mind.

"Amelia, how are you feeling?"

I grit my teeth. "Did you fucking drug me?"

"I had to. I'm sorry. I knew you wouldn't leave

the estate without a fight, and I had to get you out of there before anyone noticed."

His words say one thing, but the shackle around my wrist says another. "What the fuck is going on?"

"I'm only trying to keep you safe, Amelia."

I lift my wrist. "By chaining me to the bed."

It's hard to see his face in the faded light, but I can sort of make out a frown. "If I don't restrain you, you'll go off on your own and do something stupid. Believe me, it's for the best."

What the fuck is this guy even on? "I'm the head of the family. Unchain me right now."

"I can't do that, I'm afraid. You'll understand when all of this is over."

"When all of *what* is over?"

He tucks his hands behind his back. "Unfortunately, your mother didn't want to listen to me either. I'm only doing what's best for our family, Amelia. Please don't give me another choice. I'm telling you that I'm going to take care of it. So sit tight here and let me do that before you wind up getting yourself hurt."

"What the *fuck* are you *talking* about?" He isn't making any sense. "Uncle, you're speaking nonsense to me right now. What are you trying to do?"

"The O'Conners need to be dealt with before they get it in their heads that they can take over the Devlins. I won't let that happen, but you don't seem to care about it when it's our most pressing matter."

Jesus fuck, *this* again?

"Uncle, we've been over this."

"Yes," he snaps. "We have. And you still refuse to listen to me. So therefore, I've had to take matters into my own hands."

"By kidnapping me? You know the rest of the family is going to wonder where I am."

"I've already taken measures into taking care of that. In fact, your lawyer is going to provide the perfect alibi for you once I get my hands on him too."

My wrist stings when I jerk at the shackle trying to lunge for him. "Don't you *dare* touch him."

He chuckles softly. "Please, Amelia. Don't go growing soft on me. He's a random American. Hardly anyone will miss or coming looking for him."

That's not true, I want to scream. His sister would, that much I know. She had seemed like the type of person to go to the ends of the Earth for her brother, much like my mother and I were. We'd do anything to keep the other safe, and without actually spending any time with Jax's sister, I know she feels the same way.

That was the kind of bond you could never get back. So when you had it, you cherished it.

"Fuck you." I yank at the restraint again. "Go near him and you die."

He chuckles again. "All right, relax. Why don't I turn on some TV for you to get your mind off things? I'll be by later with some food. For now, enjoy a nice vacation away from all of this."

As he turns to walk toward the TV on the other side of the room, I can't help but yell. "Don't you care? Don't you care that you're taking your only sister's remaining child and locking her up in some dusty-ass room? Can't you see how much that would break her heart?"

My uncle sighs at me before grabbing the remote and flipping the TV on. He tabs through the channels before finding some kind of Lifetime movie and sets the remote down on top of the TV, far away from my reach.

"There. Now relax for a while and unwind. I'll be by with food later."

"You're sick," I tell him. "So fucking sick. I hope you know once I get out of this, I'm going to put a bullet in your head."

He doesn't bother to feed into the bait and walks over to the door instead to open it. "Goodbye, Amelia. I'll see you soon."

CHAPTER 25

Jax

"WHAT DO WE DO?" is the first thing that comes tumbling out of my mouth.

Aidan sets the gun down on top of Amelia's desk, his voice surprisingly calm as he says, "I'll pull up the security cams. Go ask around and see who was the last to see her."

I shake my head. "That's going to take too long and who knows when this happened?"

My mind is fucking reeling. Holy fuck, what if someone snuck onto the property and tried to kill her? What if this is the work of Aidan's family?

"We don't have any other options right now, Jax." He grabs my shoulder again in a hard hold, jostling me back from my spiraling thoughts. "We need to find out if she was taken off the property or not."

"Fuck." I swipe my clean hand over my face. "Okay...all right."

The last time I was involved in a murder plot, my

sister almost died. Am I ready to relive that shit? Over another person I care about? Whoever the fuck hurt her is going to pay; I don't care who they are or what connections they have.

If it takes getting my hands dirty, then so be it.

Aidan lets go of me, stepping back to move around to the other side of the desk. "Meet me in my room in an hour."

No one in this entire goddamn estate had any idea where Amelia could've gone.

She was like a ghost, completely disappearing without a trace at all. It was hard not to let on what was happening as I questioned the waitstaff down in the kitchen, the maid staff that were busy running up and down the halls, and the guards out in the front end of the property.

Hopefully, word didn't travel much since I'd been trying to keep my comments as vague as possible, but it was clear to me that no one had seen Amelia since late last night.

That sinking feeling in my chest didn't go away at all, growing worse as each person denied seeing her. There is no way she left without saying anything to anyone or seeing someone. That just doesn't happen to the head of a mafia family.

Especially someone like Amelia.

When I finally head up to Aidan's room, I all but

blow through the door as I enter. He merely looks up at me for a brief moment before his eyes focus back down at his computer screen.

His room is bigger than I thought it would be, though I suppose that makes sense seeing as how he's technically an heir himself. There is a small sitting area over by the three sets of windows facing the outside retaining wall along with a California king bed off in the corner with sheets that have been pulled back and pillows slightly skewed.

Over where Aidan is, he has a large double-wide desk that has three sets of monitors on it along with a computer tower that glows an ominous green from inside the glass window. On his monitors looks to be several live feeds of the outside perimeter of the estate, along with one of the street right outside of it.

"Find anything?"

"No."

My heart sinks again. *Fuck...*

"Which isn't right." His fingers tap on the keyboard, zooming in on something. "Because not an inch of this entire estate doesn't have a camera on it."

Shutting the door behind me, I head over to him. "What's that mean?"

Aidan clicks on another feed, zooming in again. "It means that whoever took her, or hurt her, knew the layout of this place."

Crossing my arms, my eyes glance over the feeds, none of them jumping out at me. They're all fairly clear with good camera quality, and true to Aidan's words, it seems like every single angle is visible. There's even a camera facing the fountain that has the angle of the drive leading up to the estate from the gates below.

"Is there a way to smuggle someone out of here underground?" I ask.

Aidan nods. "Which is why someone needed to have known the layout of this place. That kind of information isn't public knowledge, let alone a fact even someone who would've visited this place for a party or a meeting would know."

Fuck, so we really are looking at foul play.

"Where's Sean?"

Aidan cranes his neck to blink up at me. "What?"

"You said you got a weird vibe from him the other day. Where is he? He on any of these feeds?"

There's a slight pause before Aidan's turning around and clicking through a few of them. It isn't until he gets to a feed of the garage that he leans back and sighs.

"His car's gone."

"Fuck," I mutter, running my hand along my jaw. "We need to find him."

"Here's the problem with that." Aidan runs a hand through his hair, pushing it out of his face. "Say Sean did something to Amelia and took her somewhere. I think it's safe to say Amelia fought back, but obviously she was taken regardless. Which means one of two things. One, Sean brought her somewhere and is holding her. Or two, he killed her."

My blood runs cold at the last statement. "He wouldn't."

Aidan glances up at me. "What makes you so sure?"

I shake my head. Maybe I'm reading too much into things, but with the little I've had of my interactions with Sean, he's never seemed to me like an impulsive person. He seemed too calculated for him to have stuck Amelia and to have dragged her body out to run off and dump it somewhere.

Plus, with no one catching him *and* nothing being on the cameras…there had to have been some planning. Which meant he wouldn't go through the trouble of doing all of this just to take Amelia's place. If he wanted a coup, he would've just done so and killed her in front of everyone. Not make it look like she left for a day trip out into the city.

It made no sense. She had to be alive.

"Because he has no reason to kill her. If she simply goes missing, he gets every opportunity to step up as head of the family. He'll look like a hero if he finds her, and she'll look like an idiot for being captured."

"Damn." Aidan looks back at the monitors in front of him. "That's true…"

"If Sean wants head of the family that badly, he needs to be calculated about it. Killing Amelia is reckless and stupid. Not to mention it's too close to her own mother's death. Doing that is going to scare all of their contacts into thinking the Devlins are a liability. No one wants to work with a family who keeps getting their head cut off."

"True." He nods. "So we need to look for Sean."

I shake my head. "We need to wait for Sean to come back and then look for Amelia."

Aidan looks at me again.

"Making it look like we're also in the dark is going to be the only way we are going to be able to move through the shadows. Can you put a tracker on his car? He'll have to go visit her eventually if he put her somewhere where no one can find her."

He hesitates. "I can, but..."

"What? Aidan, we have to save her."

He shakes his head at me and stands. "It's not that. I want to bring her home too. The problem is that none of this is solid evidence. It's all speculation. We need to find out if any of what you're saying is close to the truth or too far off from it. We'll not only need to put a tracker on his car but bug his phone, get someone to follow him, the whole nine yards."

I'm growing frustrated the more we talk about this. We're wasting precious time that we could be using to track Amelia down.

I know she's not dead. She left Aidan that voicemail for a reason. She isn't that careless that she would pocket dial someone and leave them a minute-long voicemail without realizing it and texting about it afterward. Especially not on the day she mysteriously vanishes.

It's all too much to be a coincidence.

It has to mean something.

"Aidan."

He holds his hands up. "Look, I get you have a plan, but I'm being realistic."

"Well, then who do you trust here that can help?"

He snorts. "No one. Who knows how many people Sean has under his belt? There's no telling where Amelia's loyalty is or Sean's within this family. It's all going to be jumbled."

Fuck, what are we going to do now?!

Letting out a harsh sigh, I card my hands through my hair.

"But," Aidan speaks again, "I may have an idea."

"What?" It comes out more of a snap than a genuine question.

"I know some people that could help find her that don't run the risk of being on Sean's payroll."

"Okay, great." Rolling my wrists, I gesture for him to continue.

He frowns slightly. "It's not going to be what you want to hear."

"Aidan, I swear to god—"

"My family," he crosses his arms, "can help."

I stare at him for a long moment. "You're...not actually serious."

He shrugs. "They aren't on Sean's payroll, I can guarantee you that much."

"Why would they be interested in helping us find Amelia? This gives them more of a reason to take over while the Devlins are struggling."

"Maybe so. But you can always bargain with them."

Bargain? What in the world did I have that would give me enough buying power to ask a powerful family like the O'Conners for a favor? Not to mention I would be enlisting the help of Amelia's enemy who had no obligations to actually help.

"How, Aidan? I have nothing."

"It isn't a matter of what you do and don't have with my family. It's a matter of what you're willing to eventually do."

"Such as?"

He shrugs again. "I don't know. Your own limits are something you need to figure out. The real question is: are you willing to do anything to get her back?"

As I stare at him, I know what my answer will be. I know what it will always be because it's the same thing I did the second I realized I'd regretted leaving her at the airport to come back to Ireland all by herself.

I'd do *anything* for her, and if that meant going into the lion's den and selling myself to the highest bidder—if it got her back to me—I'd do it in a heartbeat.

Would Amelia hate me for this afterward, enlisting the help of the people trying to take her family down, or would she be happy to know that I'd got to the fucking lengths of this damn Earth in order to make sure she was safe?

I wasn't sure. But all I could do was to take the hand that had been offered to me and hope that it didn't end in me losing everything in the process.

I breathe out slowly. "Okay, I want to talk to them."

Aidan nods, his face drawn into a serious frown. "All right. Then I'll take you to them."

Before You Go...

If you enjoyed my book please leave a short review. These reviews help me as an author to be found by other amazing readers like you.

Thank you so much! :)

About J. J. Love

JJ Love is a steamy romance author who loves to write about Billionaire & Mafia Romantic Suspense.

She loves her coffee, hanging out at the beach, and traveling.

Keep up with all things Instant Billionaire here ➜ https://www.facebook.com/groups/jj.love.author

Download Mystery Woman - 12 Months Later (bonus scene from Instant Billionaire) here ➜ https://dl.bookfunnel.com/925my28kre

About Simone Fox

Simone Fox is a steamy romance author who loves to write about sexy bad boys.

When she's not working on her next book, she's traveling or hanging out with family.

Keep up with all things Lured here ➜ https://www.facebook.com/groups/simone.fox

www.ingramcontent.com/pod-product-compliance
Lightning Source LLC
LaVergne TN
LVHW091135080826
845145LV00008B/2158

* 9 7 8 1 6 4 0 3 4 6 6 4 2 *